"Rolls-Royce" of Poverty and other stories

Olusola Samuel Aina

To Jullie ABC tales
Best Regards
Sam
26/3/2014

Published by Olusola Samuel Aina

Copyright © 2013 Olusola Samuel Aina

29 Beech Rd
Dartford
DA1 2RG
UK
Olusola.S.Aina@gmail.com

ISBN:099262200X
ISBN-13:9780992622008

Dedication

To my wife, Roseline Modupe Aina

Contents

Acknowledgments

Thanks to my aunt, Mrs D T Aina, who has always been asking about my writing right from my secondary school years until now and also, Uncle John (Dr. Rev. J O Aina). These two people are the kindest, most unselfish couple I have had the good fortune to be related to.

My thanks also go to my cousin Comfort Green (Egbon Komfo) whose constant words of encouragement I have always found to be most genuine and to her husband Don, an absolute gentleman.

Many thanks also to Tai and Ayo Aina for their very kind interest and encouragement.

Also, to Serena Lee - thank you for reading through the manuscript and offering such useful suggestions.

Neeti Sharma, thanks for your suggestions and your kind and helpful comments.

And, of course, thanks to my very good friend Damian Griffiths, who read the manuscript and offered valuable suggestions on the ordering of the stories.

I must also acknowledge here the kind support and encouragement of Charles and Lisa Benjamin, a lovely and inspirational couple.

Thanks to Tony Cook, John Bird and Gordon Roddick for setting up ABCtales.com, the open writers forum where I submitted my writings for review and comments by fellow writers. Many thanks to Celticman, Blessing, Eamon and Tcook for their occasional feedback and kind comments.

I must also thank the exceptional editors who have cast their expert eye on the stories. Loraine Mace, who offered excellent suggestions on two of the stories, and also the spectacularly talented editors from Servicescape.com - WordMechanic, BuzzWord, WriteWatchman, EditrixJD and Ace-Editor.

Many, many thanks to Nick Jones of Full Media Ltd for his sterling proofreading work.

Finally, I would like to say a big thank you to the "Creatives" from crowdSPRING.com who contested for the cover design.

And a very special thanks to Paul Quarry who produced the winning cover design.

"Rolls-Royce" of Poverty

All I wanted was his wallet and his mobile phone. He shouldn't have panicked. He shouldn't have tried to make a break for it, only to turn around and put up a fight. Although he was taller than I was, and probably sixteen - like me - he had no chance against my combat skills. One moment he was swaggering along as if he owned the place, showing off his fancy phone, his trousers bulging with his wallet, with that filthy smirk on his ruddy city-boy face. Next thing you know he's squealing like a piglet, writhing in the pool of his own blood. The resounding 'Thwack!' as the stone connected with his fat, pompous head ensured he wouldn't be getting up anytime soon.

I didn't hang around.

Once I'd picked up the mobile from the ground and yanked the wallet from his pocket, I bolted into the dry bush that flanked the old footpath.

He asked for it, stupid city boy. The jelly-brained rich kid wandering into my territory, brandishing his poncey mobile phone, and waving his fat wallet around. He deserved everything he'd got. I palmed my booty and smiled; something to brag about to Ramon and the boys. It'll drive them mad with excitement.

I skipped over the open drain that crossed the path just before the makeshift thatched structure that served as the mosque.

I'd been living in the Purakija ever since I was born. It wasn't exactly a village or a town but a dwelling place of sorts. The place used to be a desolate waste site at the edge of Makimwe Township. But as Makimwe developed extremely fast, the Purakija was where the dregs of society ended up - a waste product of globalization. The Purakija consisted of clusters of small settlements populated with hundreds of corrugated iron shacks. The shacks, each measuring about seven by seven feet, were interspersed with open drains that stank of refuse and urine. "That," my father had often said, "is the smell of affluence." But that didn't stop me from constantly wrinkling my nose and holding my breath in disgust. Each shack was a single-room apartment that housed a family of three to sixteen. One of those shacks was my home, shared with my father and my mother.

I remembered the look on that boy's face the moment he saw me. There was a brief flash of panic; a sudden widening of the eyes in an expression of doomed surprise. Dancing flames of naked fear, quickly replaced by a futile bravado that prevailed until his situation became more plainly obvious. But it was that flash, that brief betrayal of vulnerability that always fascinated me. I'd seen it so many times. I'd seen it in my father's eyes sometimes, even when he was laughing.

As I approached our home, I saw that my father and Mr Abdul were engaged in a conversation. Mr Abdul was not a dweller in the Purakija. However, everybody in the area knew him because he'd grown up there. He and my father were childhood friends, so he visited regularly. I didn't like him at all. He had a patronizing attitude, and I was sure that he visited just to remind himself how his life would have turned out if he hadn't had his lucky break. He was always flaunting his wealth and boasting about his possessions.

Backtracking into the shadows, I crabbed my way round to the back of our shack. There, part of the corrugated sheet had peeled away, allowing me to creep through unspotted. I was immediately engulfed by a discomfiting warmth and the stale odour of gone-off food and dirty clothing, as I penetrated the unlit enclosure that served as our lounge, kitchen, bedroom - and, sometimes, toilet.

I took refuge under the bamboo bed that was raised at one corner with a battered wooden case that contained Mother's clothes. The only thing I loved about our home was the darkness and the solitude that I found under the bed. I'd lie there all day, lost in my dreams, inspired by images in old magazines and chance glimpses on a TV screen, or from the fantasies and yarns concocted and spun by Ramon and other members of my local district gangs.

From my vantage point under the bed, through the litter of boxes, old shoes and other mouldy junk, I could see and hear Mr Abdul and my father. Mr Abdul was enthralling him with tales of his latest trip to the United States. Still in his threadbare shorts and flay-sleeved shirt that he wore around the house, my father was gazing agape, with the rapt attention of a faithful terrier, at his friend, who was attired in satin pantaloons, embroidered native boubou and a red fez with sequins that glittered in the dying evening sunlight.

"This one is called the Statue of Liberty. People can see it many miles away…"

"What, you mean, like the great Atiba monument in the centre of Purakija market?"

Such was the level of ignorance of my father, comparing America's Statue of Liberty to the Atiba monument - a pile of junk cobbled together from scrap metal, with no hint of beauty, and which could certainly not be seen from anywhere. Everything he saw, no matter how magnificent, how awesome, had to be scaled down within the limits of his own squalid world.

"Just look at the lights in the houses and the streets; how they twinkle like the reflection of sunlight in the roadside gutters after the floods."

Mr Abdul was showing my father images in a camcorder, which he held up while my father peered and squinted over his friend's left shoulder.

"That house must be bigger than the house of the municipal councillor, just outside the Pura."

"Yes, of course, that is called the Empire State Building."

My whole body crawled with shame and embar-rassment at my father's small-mindedness. The stuff he

4

was admiring in that camcorder was beyond the limits of his comprehension. He couldn't see the appalling contrast between the beautiful streets, the marvellous buildings and the magnificent cars shown to him in the video, with the filth that surrounded him. His mind was stuck in the odious mud of his immediate squalor and his hopeless ignorance. Despite his impoverishment, everything around him remained beautiful and perfect in his own eyes. He cruised the highway of disgrace and embarrassment in his Rolls-Royce of poverty.

Deciding that I'd had enough, I started towards the rear exit, but I was stopped in my tracks by what Mr Abdul said next, and I crawled back under the bed.

"Look, my dear friend Daud, look what I brought you from the States." He passed a white cardboard box, which had been out of view until then, to my father, who accepted it with a curious mixture of gratitude and surprise. His hands trembled as he opened the box and gingerly lifted out its contents with the care with which he would have handled a new-born baby. They were a pair of white plimsoll shoes.

"Aaaah!" His eyes were wide with wonder and pleasure. "Angel shoes!" he whispered.

I almost burst out in laughter.

What a stupid gift! I couldn't see my father wearing them in a million years, but he was overwhelmed by his friend's generosity. His eyes glistened with joy and excitement, and he genuflected in front of his friend with the fervour of an apprentice ironsmith working the bellows.

Long after Mr Abdul had said his farewell and departed, my father stood in the doorway, still cradling his prize. Only much later did he suddenly snap out of his stupor and put them away under the bed, almost poking my eye out with the corner of the box as he shoved it far underneath.

My father was sitting on the floor with his back to the front wall, playing his flute, when Mother arrived from the cassava farms where she had been toiling all day. The farms were so far away that it took more than two hours to get there; two hours walking barefoot on the baking hot gravelly path that wound steeply up and down the savage hills of Makimwe.

She slowly lowered the huge basket that she had been carrying on her head. It contained a few skinny cassava tubers and some corncobs. But the bulk of her burden was the hand-operated grinding equipment that was essential to her work in the farms. It was no use in the house, but she couldn't leave it out there for fear that it would be stolen or vandalized. So she had to lug that chunky beast all the way to and from the farms every day.

Mother immediately set about making some cassava porridge for our dinner. Dinner was the only real meal we had; other than that, we had to make do during the day with any sort of snack that came our way.

I remained in my hideout for most of the evening. I could hear the undulating mutter of my father's voice as he whined between mouthfuls. He hadn't made any money from his busking. He'd been out there fluting all day in the heat of the sun, and he hadn't received a single penny. It seemed to him that people were becoming meaner and stingier.

Mother's ensuing laugh was not the sort with which people reacted to something funny. It was a sad laugh, the sort that didn't make the other person laugh back.

"Don't you think you should be doing a proper job - working on the farm, peddling a real trade, or joining the labourers on the building sites in the township? The farm hands at Kikawa take home no less than 50 shillings after a hard day's work. I'm telling you, Daud, one of these days... One of these days..." But she could never bring herself to complete her threat, and my father never pressed her further.

I'd heard Mother often complain that life in the Pura was not fit even for a dog. It was her greatest shame and sadness that she'd found herself living in such a wretched place. Her disaffection had increased by leaps and bounds recently, and when she started her tirade it was like an unstoppable deluge.

My father quietly continued to eat his porridge, deadpan. But even after he finished his food, mother kept at him without letting up.

"Aren't you just a little bit ashamed of yourself? How many real men would stay home all day while their wife goes out to make a living...?"

He fiddled nervously with his flute and then, after a while, he said, "Well, I'm sure you know that God's time is the best," which, as usual, did the trick. That magic phrase was his faithful escape clause. It always shut her up because she was deeply religious. Her father was a catechist and her mother was a catechist's daughter. She never missed Sunday service, and she unfailingly tithed her meagre earnings to her local church in cash or in kind. So, when my father played the God card, it was always a sure banker. It left her crestfallen, sitting in the corner on an upturned pail that was only good for sitting on. She starred glumly at my father.

The newly-restored calm prevailed for a short while, during which the tension slowly evaporated. At this point, my father felt safe enough to broach the matter that had been exciting him all day.

"Abdul was here earlier."

He weighed up her initial silence and proceeded cautiously, watching her face for the glow of delight and wonderment he was sure he'd see after he'd told her all about it.

"He's only just arrived from America, where he's been to see his son, Lawal."

"Hmm…"

Emboldened by the seemingly positive reaction, he continued. "He brought pictures - motion pictures in a small transistor radio, the thing was like… like a small television. You should have seen the fabulous life that they live out there."

"Hmm…"

"Yes, I too was astounded. The roads are wider than the Mulamkiwe stream… Everyone lived in white mansions, and you should see the cars…the cars! They're like… like… nothing you've ever seen before."

As she hadn't uttered a single word, he assumed that she had been awed into silence by his description of the foreign scenes and fabulous lifestyle overseas.

"Let me show you what Abdul brought back for me." He rushed away and returned with the shoes, which he lifted very carefully out of the box and cradled possessively. "Look! Aren't they just delightful?"

Mother didn't share any of his excitement. She sat on her feet, and her shoulders heaved as she began to weep.

"Why, what's the matter?"

Lips pursed, eyes deep and sullen, she just rocked back and forth as if she was in the throes of grief.

My father moved closer and touched her shoulder, but she swatted his hand away as if it were an annoying fly.

He stood there holding the shoes, staring sheepishly at the floor, then put them away, quietly took up his flute and waddled out of the shack, back to the barber's shed where he whiled away his time, lounging there with other men of his hapless, wasted ilk.

The sight of Mother crying had become more frequent in recent weeks, and I no longer found it so unnerving. But I still had no words to say to her under these circumstances. I only guessed it might help if at least she knew I was there. So I crawled out of hiding and sat next to her. After a while, I became bored and felt awkward about the whole thing, so I got up and headed for the door. But just as I was about to escape, she called after me.

"Rafik, you haven't had something to eat."

My cassava porridge was in a small bowl beneath the square hole cut into the corrugated wall, which served as the main window. The cassava was still warm, but I wasn't hungry. I swallowed each morsel without tasting it.

"How was school today?"

"Fine." My response was involuntary - a programmed reply to any question relating to school. If I'd been asked that question in my sleep, I'd have given exactly the same answer, even though I'd not been to school for longer than I cared to remember. And it didn't matter, either, that she knew I was lying. I couldn't understand the whole point of school when there was only one teacher for more than ninety of us. And the dirty old jerk was drunk most of the time. All he ever did was harass the students and molest the older girls. I doubted very much whether a single word of knowledge or wisdom had ever crossed his wretched lips.

I could feel Mother watching me as I ate. She sighed. "You must not become like your father. You must learn a respectable trade and work very hard so that you can escape this miserable place."

After that, she busied herself about the shack, moving things around and sweeping out the dust. There didn't seem to be any sense in her activities. Whatever she did, everything always remained the same. The floor was still dusty, the walls were still covered in grime and rust, and the place still stank.

By the time I'd finished my porridge and licked my bowl clean, Mother had perked up, and I could hear her humming a cheerful church chorus. I went under the bed, gathered my father's new plimsolls, and quietly slipped out of the front door.

"Where did you get those?" Ramon's eyes were wider than the dyeing pools of Batamwe. We were in back districts of the Pura, where the black oily Mulamkiwe stream deposited waste from the township, a place where scrap iron was dumped in massive heaps. Our usual hangout was near one of the piles of scrap. Here, we were shielded from the other gangs that roamed around, or gathered near the piles of scrap that they preferred. I did a fanciful catwalk up and down a small clearing in front of Ramon and two other guys.

"My father bought them for me," I declared.

They all burst out into an unexpected cacophony of raucous laughter, falling over one another, which went on for quite some time.

"I bet you stole them," Ramon jeered.

"No. I assure you that they belong to my father, but these..." I said, magically conjuring the wallet and the mobile phone concealed in the pockets of my oversized shorts, "...I stole." I savoured the sudden change of expression that came upon their faces, mouths agape and hungry eyes widening, twinkling in their hollow sockets like the dying glow of a torchlight running out of battery power.

But my moment of glory was short-lived.

I soon realized, all too late, that we were not there alone. Ayana, whom everyone called 'the vulture', was lurking around. He was one of the most odious characters in the neighbourhood. Ayana was always picking on the younger gangsters to please the older ones because he was not accepted by any gang. It was not because of his age, height or any other obvious reason, but just because of how he was.

"How kind of you to be looking after my precious possessions in my absence," his voice boomed from behind me. I turned round sharply and glowered at him. He was leaning on the free-standing carcass of what could once have been part of a brand new Toyota Hiace. He sauntered lazily over and stretched out a long scrawny hand, suddenly harshening his voice. "C'mon, squirt, don't be slow in handing them over."

I stared at him, but not for too long. It was no use, of course. If I resisted, it would only take one word to the grand junta, and I was as good as dead. These guys never messed about. The life of a young man in these parts can be bitter and short if he kicks against established authority. There'd been too many examples, and I was not eager to be added to that list. My moment of glory had come and gone, and I had no huge misgivings over my loss. Ayana snatched the items with a swift movement of his hand and then jerked his crooked face at us in one final show of villainy.

When we were sure he'd gone, Ramon stood up. "Rafik, you're chicken. You shouldn't have let him take all that stuff from you like that."

But I only grimaced and shrugged. "Easy come, easy go."

It was very late when I got back to our shack. I expected that my father would be asleep, so I tried to creep in to lie on the small raffia mat close to the door.

"Where have you been? Do you know how late it is?" my father's voice boomed from somewhere in the darkness, causing me to stumble.

"I was in Ramon's house; I overslept." I congratulated myself on the ease and promptness with which I thought up such a plausible excuse. I was such a competent fibber.

He didn't say anything for a while, and I just about managed to feel my way to the place where my sleeping mat was before he stopped me in my tracks...

"Where's my new shoes, Rafik?"

But I was ready for that one. "What shoes? I haven't seen any shoes."

Silence, again. Which was uncharacteristic of my father; he was normally threatening and cursing. But this time, nothing more was said. I promptly fell into a gratefully sound sleep.

The following morning, I woke up at about 6:30 and went through the motions of preparing for school, which I had no intention of attending. Mother had already set off on her gruelling marathon trek to the cassava farms. My father was still in bed. He was often still in bed by the time I set out for school. But, of course, I did not go to school. I hung around the Puja with the lads until late in the afternoon and then generally had a wander about town.

Later in the afternoon, after the sun had spent up the worst of its sting, I was on my way back from my adventures. As I passed the place where I'd thrashed that stupid rich prat, I looked around furtively and hastened my pace. But suddenly I heard footsteps behind me and walked faster. To turn around would be to betray my fear. The footsteps sounded closer and faster, and it was soon obvious that I should break into a run. But, just as I took off, the person behind me shouted "Thief!" which filled me with dread because, in these Purakija slums, instant justice was the thing that prevailed. At the first shout of "Thief", the vigilantes would spill out of nowhere and come after you. When they caught up with you, what you got was the necklace of fire.

"Thief, thief! I saw you yesterday...it was you...thief!"

I ran faster than I'd ever run, but my assailant wasn't doing too badly either. He didn't relent in his pace, not once, and his deafening shouts of accusation did not decrease. My luck lasted only as long as my energy. Soon he was joined by more pursuers, and I had no chance when the mob descended on me, baying like a pack of bloodthirsty hounds.

Someone grabbed me by my shirt lapels in a grip so tight I was starting to choke. Another one locked my hands behind my back and dragged me down the dirt path towards the central square, against my feeble protestations.

"If you're not a thief, why did you run?" asked the man who had me by my lapels, above the thundering chorus of "Thief, thief, thief..." There must have been up to fifty of them. I looked in their faces, in their eyes, for mercy, but all I saw was hatred and vengefulness. Although some of them looked familiar, no-one seemed to have any inclination to appeal on my behalf. I felt a sharp pain on my calves where a thin, red-eyed boy in oily rags was whipping at me with a long, thorny stick, his eyes glowing with a crazed glee.

But just as I was about to give up and resign myself to my doom, a sharp, authoritative voice cut through the frenzy. "Stop, stop, stop, please. Let the boy go." I immediately recognized the voice of my savior.

Mr Abdul!

"I know him well, and I can tell you that he is not a thief."

"But I saw him yesterday," said the man who had me by the lapels. "He beat up a young man, stole from him and ran away before I could catch him."

"It couldn't have been me," I cried, "I wasn't even anywhere near here yesterday..."

"I'd vouch for him like my own son," said Mr Abdul. "He wouldn't do any such thing."

I felt the grip loosen.

The mob slowly fell back and dispersed, leaving only Mr Abdul and me. I regarded him with gratitude. He'd saved my life.

The plaintive wail of my father's flute greeted me from a

distance. It had a particular melancholy quality that I hadn't noticed before. When I saw him sitting in the doorway, shoulders slumped, his head bowed and tilted to the side, and his eyes glittering, I knew something was amiss. He moved aside slowly to let me into the shack without interrupting his sad racket.

Mother hadn't returned from the cassava farms, and there wasn't a single scrap of food anywhere in the shack. I crawled into my usual hideout under the bed, lay on my stomach and closed my eyes. But I couldn't drift into my magic world. The rodents of starvation were gnawing away in my stomach; it felt as if they were making mincement of my guts. I went and sat beside my father and stared out into the slum.

His eyes were shut, and his thin dry lips wrapped around the mouthpiece of his flute twitched gently as he breathed out each note. I heard loud growls, but I couldn't tell whether they were coming from his stomach or mine.

He stopped and looked at me for the first time.

"Yesterday, she left. She said she'd had enough, and she's gone back to her father's house in Wariri."

I felt a hard lump ascend my gullet and explode in my larynx. For several minutes I sobbed, and my eyes hurt from the salt in my tears.

That night, we went to sleep without anything to eat, and I dreamt I was being chased by a seven-headed monster with fire for tongues and rocks for eyes.

For the first time as far as I could remember, my father was up before sunrise. He paced about in the dark, and glanced out of the window from time to time as if he was determined to be the first to catch a glimpse of the morning's rays.

I didn't have to pretend to go to school. Instead, we set out for some place that my father did not tell me about, but judging from the purposefulness of his strides and determination in his eyes, I was sure he had a specific destination in mind. We came out of the Pura and carried on along the pitted road that led to the township. I'd never been that far out. We walked on for over an hour and a half before we finally came to a stop in front of a sumptuous white building surrounded by concrete walls with large coils of barbed wire on top. There was a massive gate, a small pedestrian entrance and a cubicle where a uniformed attendant sat. His green khaki shirt and trousers were clean but they were faded and threadbare at the elbows and knees.

We stood before the gates and the attendant came out and stared stonily at us while my father explained that we were there to see Mr Abdul. We waited for a few minutes while he consulted with somebody in the house through a wall-mounted speaker, and then turned round. "Master is not in at the moment, and we are not aware that he is expecting you at this time."

My father said, "We're prepared to wait out here until he returns."

The guard started to say something but stopped and just said, "OK, please yourself," before going back into his little office.

There was nowhere to sit. We remained standing

for over an hour, and I was quite relieved when a white BMW with tinted windows arrived. Mr Abdul wound down the window and popped his head out.

"Daud, what are you doing here?" The shriek in his voice indicated alarm, rather than surprise. Perhaps he never expected the squalor of the slum to catch up with him in his world of comfort and luxury, preferring rather to visit it on his own terms, and at his leisure.

He stepped out of the car and then turned angrily to the guard. "For goodness sake, why did you not let them in?"

He cast a benevolent glance in my direction, and we walked with him to the house while he carried on chatting with my father.

As soon as we were seated in Mr Abdul's spacious lounge, my father told his friend that he'd resolved to do something about his situation. He needed some money to start a small trade in cocoa and kola nuts. He went on about his past hardships and how he had constantly been eluded by fortune. He was at his wits' end.

"I just can't take it any more… I must do whatever I have to do to turn my life around…and for this, I really need your help."

Mr Abdul listened without once taking his eyes off my father's face. He remained silent for a long time afterwards, appearing to be in deep thought. At some point, I was wondering if he'd gone into a trance. But he spoke eventually, after what seemed like forever. "OK, I will do everything I can to help you. What sort of a friend would I be otherwise? I'll loan you some money to start your trade, and I'll see what I can do about putting some business your way."

My father rubbed his hands together. "That would be fantastic. I'll make sure that I return every penny to you. You'll never regret this, I swear."

And then Mr Abdul said, "Perhaps Rafik should stay here with us in the meantime. I need more hands at the saw mill, and there is a lot he could be helping with around here. Once the loan is repaid, he will return to you."

My father's eyes glistened, and his voice carried a fatigued rasp. He stooped slightly and gazed at the floor. He seemed completely overwhelmed with relief and gratitude. "Of course, Abdul, I swear to you on my mother's life, one day I will pay you back for this." Then he glanced at me briefly, but he did not catch my eye.

Mr Abdul patted me on the shoulder and smiled at me. "Don't worry, Rafik, I assure you that you will be very much at home here. I have no doubt that you will behave yourself, and you will not let your father or me down."

My heart sank at the thought of losing touch with all my friends back in the Pura, but at the same time, I realized that this was a positive change for me in the long run.

"You'll be sharing a room with my nephew, Mashood, who is just about the same age as you. Your first task is to look after him, as he is currently recovering from an accident."

He led me to a large, immaculate room filled with a

soft, sweet scent. There was a bed in the corner and someone was lying on it with his head bandaged. His eyes were closed, and he was still.

Mr Abdul's voice deepened slightly, and suddenly seemed resigned. "He hasn't opened his eyes since the accident." He gently brushed his hand on the forehead of the bed-ridden young man. "He got beaten up like this all because he was carrying an empty wallet and a fake mobile phone."

Stranger in the House

Right from the start, it had all the markings of a doomed holiday. Perhaps it was because we had tempted fate by setting out on Friday the 13th, but at the time any notion of superstition paled into insignificance when Dad discovered the flights that day were the cheapest available.

Departure day started out badly because Dad forgot to set the alarm, and we all slept beyond 7 am, an hour after our pre-arranged wake-up call. We were supposed be out of the house by 7:30, but in the end we didn't leave until 8:30. Then we were hit by another stroke of rotten luck: less than a mile from our house our beleaguered jalopy, an old Renault 11 that was meant to transport us to Gatwick Airport, suddenly broke down in a strange fit of rattling and coughing.

"Damn!" Dad swore for the hundredth time that morning. We all suspected he was going to swear a lot more in the following hours and days. "I bet that's the gasket gone."

"Feels more like a flat to me," muttered Mum, who was driving the car, but then, after a thought, she said, "I'm sure you're right, Fred. It must be the gasket."

Mum was the only one of the four of us who wasn't stressed out. She was always a pillar of strength and calm. Always in control of the situation.

Cherry, my teenage elder sister, was already as taut as Keith Richards' guitar string. She sat behind Dad, strangely quiet and sullenly resigned to the conviction that we weren't going to make it to Gatwick in time for the flight. She'd looked forward to this holiday in Spain more than the rest of us. Our long-awaited dream destination was a self-contained cabin on the outskirts of Xativa that held the promise of sunshine, fun and an unforgettable holiday. Mum and Dad had scrimped and saved for it over the past two years.

I too had earlier caved in under pressure when Dad shouted at me for taking too long in the bathroom. We hadn't even left Tunbridge Wells, and I already felt feverish and hot with apprehension and nervous tension.

The rattling increased, and the car shuddered to a halt by the curb in front of Mr Choudary's newsagent shop. Mum got out and walked round the back of the car. Dad wound down his side window and peered out.

"It's one of the back tyres!" Mum shouted. "It's as

flat as a pancake!"

Cherry jumped out of the car before I did, and then Dad reluctantly pushed the creaking door open and emerged, his face red, his lips pursed in frustration and disappointment.

Mum went into the newsagent's and came out, followed by Mr Choudary, who immediately sized up the situation and quickly set about changing the wheel. Mum thanked the middle-aged shopkeeper profusely, and after a brief grunt of acknowledgement from Dad, we all piled back into the jalopy and were on our way again.

As we passed Sevenoaks and blended with the flow of traffic on the M25, Dad switched on the radio for the third time, forgetting again that the knob was jammed and that the radio could not be tuned to any station. Cherry turned her head and stared at the passing cars, a deep frown expressing her irritation at the unwelcome radio static. Dad gave up. He switched off the radio and then started tapping the dashboard with his fingers to the rhythm of music in his head. The cool spring breeze flowed through the half-open car windows as we sped steadily towards Gatwick.

Since we'd set off from Tunbridge Wells, there'd been a whiff of electrics and stale exhaust fumes, which we hadn't paid any attention to. But this smell gradually increased and was starting to be bothersome. Cherry was the first to break the silence.

"Smells like the engine is burning," she said, matter-of-factly.

"It's OK," Dad said, "it's just 'priming' up. This old tub should get us to Gatwick alright."

Thick black smoke billowed out of the exhaust and clouded the rear view. It felt as if we were in a rocket about to take off at any moment.

"For goodness sake, Mary, what are you stopping for?" Dad exclaimed, as Mum pulled up on the hard shoulder.

But before Mum could reply, there was a loud explosion under the bonnet. Cherry screamed, Dad looked dazed and startled, but Mum reacted with mild surprise, her usual calm demeanour intact. She skipped out of the car. "Get out, guys. Don't just sit there and choke to death!"

We all stood away from the pillar of cloud that just moments before had been our transport. We'd borrowed the Renault from Kelly, our elderly neighbour three doors away. Although he hadn't used it for a long time, Dad was pleased when he discovered the engine started on the first go. He'd listened to the engine and declared it roadworthy; at least we'd save on transport to and from the airport. Dad couldn't drive because he was on disability benefit. It would cost him his allowance and other benefits if he was to be seen driving. And that was a considerable chunk of our household income.

Dad drew the mobile from his trouser pocket, took one look at it and swore. "Damn! This thing isn't charged. How are we going to call for help?"

"It's okay," said Mum. "There are always rescue patrols on the motorway around this time..."

As if on cue, a recovery truck appeared in the distance. It was likely he'd driven past us earlier and, sensing we'd soon be in trouble, he'd stuck close by somehow. A burly Irishman in blue oily overalls climbed out of his truck and strode towards us. He nodded curtly at us and then turned to Dad.

"What have we here then, eh?"

He and Dad conferred briefly before the man agreed to tow the car to the nearest service station, which was about five miles away.

Once all the smoke had cleared, the recovery man secured the towline, and we stuffed ourselves back into the Renault. I heard Dad saying to Mum over the noise of the truck's engine, "We'll be cutting this pile of junk loose at the service station. As soon as we get there, call for a taxi to take us to the airport. With a bit of luck, if we check in quickly, we might still catch the flight."

Dad regained some of his usual sense of humour, because he joked as the taxi approached, "Trust your mum to go for the bloke with the biggest beard."

"Come on, Dad!" Cherry chided. "It's not like he's going to be driving with his beard."

"Well, just so long as his beard doesn't get in the way... We've had our fair share of trouble already."

It was one of those bus taxis, with plenty of room for our luggage. Dad stood by while we put all the bags in the boot. The bearded Asian taxi driver helped us put the heavy ones away.

We proceeded to Gatwick, but not without another glitch - the driver missed Junction 7 on the M25, and had to turn back on to the motorway at a roundabout further ahead. When Dad realized this, he blew his top and started swearing. Mum rested her hand gently on his clenched fists as he rained verbal abuse on the back of the taxi driver's neck.

The tension and resentment prevailed until we finally reached the airport, with only ten minutes to check in. Dad was a nervous wreck; his face was drawn and his shoulders hunched. Cherry was a ghost of her normal sulky but confident self. Her freckled face was a picture of despondence. All her dreams of the sunny beach were hanging by a fuse wire that was going to fizzle out in ten minutes.

"Quick, guys, let's go. There's still some time!" Mum urged us out of the taxi in her calm, reassuring voice. But even Mum was slightly miffed when she saw the queue at the check-in area. My backpack suddenly felt a lot heavier, and I shed it in dismay. Cherry also dumped her bag, and Dad groaned in despair.

"Hey, look!" shouted Mum, pointing at the information screen ahead. "Our flight doesn't leave until 12:30."

"Ha, the AZ00133," said Dad, squinting at the tickets in his hands and scowling at the screen. "Of course, our outward flight is at 12:30. I must have misread." He heaved a sigh of relief.

"Dad!" Cherry reprimanded, colour coming back to her face.

"Baa…" said Dad, smiling sheepishly.

"Right, guys, let's get ourselves checked in and then

treat ourselves to a decent brunch before…" Mum was saying, her sentence cut short by Cherry giggling uncontrollably. I turned in the direction of her gaze and soon realized it was not sheer relief that had turned her into a hyena. A man in his late forties had just stepped out of the lift. He had a mop of mottled grey hair and a chubby face that oozed sweat as he struggled with a massive leather box. With his short fat legs and arms, his undersized summer shirt and his ridiculous baggy shorts, he looked grotesquely hilarious.

"Don't stare, children," Mum commanded, her voice betraying a tinkle of amusement.

"Look," Cherry whispered, half covering her mouth, "he's coming towards us."

I could hear his labored breathing as he approached, his luggage making a scraping noise on the polished floor. Finally, he stopped right next to Dad. Panting and wheezing, he placed a fat moist hand on Dad's shoulder.

"Phew! Tim, there you are at last! I knew I'd find you here."

Dad stared at him blankly and then brushed the man's hand away. "You're mistaken, matey. I don't know you."

Cherry stepped behind Dad; Mum just stared.

"Tim, I'm your brother, Frank. I may have changed a wee bit, but I'm Frank… Big brother Frank… eh?" he chuckled. "Funny turning up on you like this, eh?"

But by this time, Dad was more than irritated. All the stress of the past hours had worn him out, and he'd completely run out of patience.

"Look here, matey. I'm not your Tim, and I have never seen you before. If you don't leave me and my family alone, I will..." Dad's raised voice had an edge to it that could have sliced through concrete. Mum put her hand on his shoulder.

The man seemed to sober up and looked as if he was going to break down in tears. Mum stared at Dad, her eyebrows angled in confusion. True, she'd never met any of Dad's direct relatives since Dad had been through foster homes, and been adopted and re-adopted several times. I didn't know whether we had any uncles or aunts out there. I didn't know what it was, but something was communicated between Mum and Dad that caused Dad to calm down.

The man looked at Mum, silently pleading for her to intercede on his behalf. "I'm his brother; I'm Frank." He even turned to me, but he could not reach Cherry, who was peering from behind Dad in sheer horror. "Mate, I'm your uncle. I'm Uncle Frank." His voice was close to breaking point.

"I don't know who you are, and I'm not called Tim."

"OK, it's been a long time. Maybe you changed your name, who knows...?"

"Right," interjected Mum, "I'm sure we can sort this out..."

"Dad told me you now live in Reginald Estate, in Tunbridge Wells."

"Dad? What dad? I never knew my dad!"

"You were just a toddler when..."

"If he knew about me... If he knew where I was all these years, why the hell didn't he make contact?"

"He's seriously ill, Tim. He's got Alzheimer's..."

"I'm not Tim, for Christ's sake!"

All the while, Mum stood between them, her face a curious mixture of worry and confusion. She looked from one to the other as they batted their words back and forth. Other people around were beginning to take interest, casting uncertain glances in our direction, pulling faces and quickly looking away.

"Okay," Mum said, trying again to defuse the situation, "we can work this thing out, right?" She stared steadily at Dad, pleading for him to calm down, even if only to avoid the unpleasantness of a scene at the airport. The sooner Dad acknowledged the guy, the sooner the whole thing would blow over, and he'd be out of our hair. Dad began to say something, but he just let it trail off when he finally caught Mum's eye.

The man seemed to cheer up a little bit, but Dad's face remained as hard as granite.

"Look, I don't blame you for not wanting to have anything to do with me after what I've done. But that was more than forty years ago... I'm a changed man... All I ask is a chance to get to know you and your family, and to bond with my lovely niece and nephew."

This caused Cherry to shriek and cling to Dad more tightly. I, likewise, kept a safe distance from this weird stranger.

Eventually, after the war of words, Dad resigned -

thoroughly beaten and subdued. "OK," Dad shrugged. "So, what next?"

None of us was prepared for Frank's next words, which he said rubbing his pudgy hands together and switching to a wolfish smile.

"I'm coming with you guys."

Mum was the first to recover. "Don't be silly," she said.

"Of course, I got my return ticket to Valencia from the same online agent you got yours from."

"But how did you ..."

He tapped the side of his nose in a telling gesture. "Got it all off the database. You'd be surprised what you can find out with a little bit of hacking and poking around on the internet."

Mum's face paled visibly, she was obviously out of her depth. She'd seen something on the man's face that had unnerved her. I'd seen it too, a psychotic grin that came and went in a flash. But Mum was quick to regain most of her normal composure just in time to handle Dad's next wave of temper.

"You're not coming near me or any of my family!" Dad growled, pointing a menacing finger into Frank's face.

"Come on, guys." The man sobered up again, his small, deep-set eyes glistening, his voice hoarse with pleading and his face crumpled like that of a wounded grizzly bear.

Cherry, still hiding behind Dad, was going into a fit of spasmodic sniffing. This holiday was just one nightmare after another, and we hadn't even left Gatwick yet. It was clear even to me that we were stuck with this fat, smelly heap of jelly who called himself our uncle. After all, we had no right to insist on who got on board the plane.

Dad eased off just a bit, and we proceeded to the check-in desk. His eyes darted from side to side like a couple of gerbils in an electrified cage. It was obvious he was contemplating some exit strategy for our unwanted new relative. Perhaps we could steal Frank's passport and lock him up in one of the toilets, or buy him enough beers to make him as drunk as a skunk so he could be declared unfit to get on the plane. Or we could put some of Cherry's hair shampoo in his drink; make him sick, and then call an ambulance to cart him off the scene.

When Mum handed our passports to the smartly-dressed attendant at the counter, Frank also handed in his passport, and shouted, "We're all together."

Once we'd disposed of all our luggage, Frank heartily declared, "Come now, new family of mine, let me treat you to a pre-flight meal." This seemed to thaw Dad's icy disposition, and caused him to cheer up slightly.

We took one of the bigger tables at *Amy's Restaurant*, with Frank at one end and Cherry sitting farthest away from him. We all had chicken nuggets, chips and coke, except Frank, who, in addition to that, had two large beefburgers, three sausage rolls, a big chunk of cheesecake, a couple of jam doughnuts and a milkshake. He looked more at home than Dad or Mum, who gaped at him as he talked between mouthfuls about his time in the army. After he cleaned up the last piece from his plate, he smiled contentedly and belched loudly. Even Dad flinched.

In the plane, Frank jabbered on relentlessly to the back of Dad's unyielding head throughout the two-hour flight in the Boeing 737. Cherry and I sat with Mum on the other side of the aisle and could still smell Frank's noisome whiff from there. When Mum went towards the toilet, Dad followed her, and I could see them clearly discussing our current dilemma in a frenzied, conspiratorial manner. Dad looked more reassured when he returned to his seat, and spent the rest of the flight staring out of the window.

As soon as we reached Valencia, we wasted no time getting out of the plane. By some unspoken agreement, some tacit signal, we marched on resolutely, getting a head start on the queue to clear customs, retrieve our luggage and escape before Frank could drag himself out of the plane. Frank was nowhere in sight when we retrieved our luggage from the conveyor belt. Dad put all the heavy boxes on a single trolley at lightning speed and pushed it through the exit.

The place was hot, and the air filled with the buzz of a foreign language. The sunlight glanced off Cherry's black curly hair, and her face glowed as she was preparing to enjoy the holiday at last. Mum and Dad were smiling too.

We found the bus service for Goldcar, and the bus took us to the drop-off station where we were united with the dainty blue Citroen Picasso Mum had rented over the internet for our three days in Spain.

I helped Mum load the luggage into the back while a gentleman in brown khaki shorts and short sleeves helped put the big leather suitcase in. Dad was fiddling with the TomTom GPS he'd borrowed from Bob, our next-door neighbour. He entered the name of our destination, Llocnou d'en Fenollet. We'd follow the motorway to Xativa, and the whole trip would take 43 minutes on the recommended route.

A fresh busload of Goldcar customers arrived and, to our utter dismay, a sweaty, red-faced Frank rolled out of the bus, looking like an enormous hog on a spit. He was dragging his massive leather bag behind him and gasping for breath at every step.

Dad looked as if a mule had kicked him in the stomach. He opened his mouth to say something, but nothing came out. Cherry's face clouded over, her eyes widened in horror, and she began to sniff uncontrollably. But Mum, as usual, took the impending disaster in her stride, and even managed a smile.

Frank dragged his burden to the car and then, with one final, monumental effort, he heaved it into the open boot. Dad made a belated attempt to intercept him. However, realizing that physically he was no match for this hunk of lard, he stopped short a few feet from him. Frank forced a smile and, in an attempt to be amicable, walked forward and slapped Dad on the shoulder so forcefully that he went reeling backwards in pain.

"Phew!" Frank said, "I thought I'd lost you guys.

For a moment there, I thought I'd have to find my way to our cabin in Llocnou."

"How on earth did you know about the cabin?" Dad finally found his voice, although it didn't sound anything like his.

"I already told you, Tim." Frank's smile broadened, "There's nothing on any database I can't get my hands on. A little bit of hacking and poking around on the internet - that's all it takes."

"Look, I'm telling you for the last time. Leave me alone, and leave my family alone. I don't know you, and I don't want anything to do with you," Dad lamented with helpless fury.

Frank put on a feigned hurt bear look that made him appear more ridiculous than he already was. Eventually, in utter exasperation, Dad's shoulders suddenly sagged and he finally backed down. Dad went round to the front and cast himself heavily on to the passenger seat.

"Come on, fine family of mine, let's hit the road!" Frank cheered, getting into the back seat and immediately causing one side of the car to slouch. I climbed through the other door. Cherry refused to budge. She just stood rooted to the spot, clenching and unclenching her fists. Her jaws were set in a fierce crocodile clamp, and her eyes glowed defiantly. Nothing happened until Dad finally said, "OK, Cherry, you sit in the front with your Mum, and I'll sit at the back."

Frank managed to shut the car door after five attempts. I was sandwiched between him and Dad, and it was not a happy place to be. I felt like the hide bag in the grip of an overenthusiastic amateur bagpiper. Worse still was the suffocating pong of Frank's body odour and garlic breath.

Mum manoeuvred out on to the main road and fired the Citroen towards the motorway. Dad wedged the TomTom GPS between the lips of the dashboard, next to the speedometer. The gadget displayed a reassuring continuous blue line that was supposed to be our route to Xativa. As Mum had never driven outside the UK and was concerned she might forget to drive on the right side of the road, she wore Dad's old leather watch on her right hand to serve as a constant reminder.

Twenty minutes later Dad was swearing again; the TomTom had gone blank. The battery had gone flat, and the cigarette lighter socket charger was in one of the boxes in the car boot.

"It's okay," said Mum, "We'll just follow the signs. You guys, keep your eyes open for the exit to Xativa."

"I've got a map," yawned Frank, suddenly waking up from his noisy nap, "but it's in my suitcase in the back." Then he snorted, coughed, shifted his massive bottom and went back to sleep.

But it was all straightforward, and there were no incidents all the way to Xativa. We followed the signs to Llocnou, which was only about six miles further on. Mum drifted to the wrong side after a bend on the narrow gravel road, and we just avoided a head-on collision with a yellow Volvo dump truck. As we passed, the driver waved wildly and let off a rapid burst of Spanish. None of us understood Spanish but his expression left us in no doubt about the meaning.

We finally arrived at our holiday accommodation just outside Llocnou - a pleasant compound consisting of three cabin houses and an old bungalow, which belonged to the caretaker, Mick, who met us there and showed us round. The place was dotted with massive trees, and the air was thick with the buzzing noise of strange insects.

Cherry escaped to the swimming pool shortly after we'd unpacked. Frank was lying on the sofa, still wearing his shoes. Dad was trying to work the TV and Mum was in the kitchen, surveying the view through the back window. I was beginning to get bored, so I changed into my swimming shorts and went to the pool too. I knew Cherry didn't care much for my company. We were constantly getting into a quarrel, and she'd stated that she was going to ignore me throughout the holiday. So far, she was doing a fantastic job of it, and I was not keen to rob her of the credit.

I took to the shallow end where I wallowed in the cool water and enjoyed the heat of the blazing sun. I amused myself with a red five-foot pool noodle from the utility room. I was unaware that Frank had arrived on the scene until he was in mid-flight of an awesome belly flop. He landed with a splash that sent half of the water out of the pool, and then he floundered about like a WWE wrestler in an agonising reverse chin lock. Cherry screamed, leapt out of the pool, gathered her things, and fled back to the cabin, wailing. I stepped out of the pool and followed her, looking back to see Frank floating on his back, his pock-marked face blemished further by an idiotic grin.

"Quick, put on your clothes," Dad said, almost in a whisper as I entered the cabin. "We're all going out and we're leaving Uncle Kong here by himself."

Frank didn't appear to notice as we drove out of the compound with bated breath. As we turned into the small road towards Xativa I glanced at Dad. His faced glowed triumphantly. "We'll look for a restaurant in town and have some tapas."

"I'll have paella!" Cherry chirped, smiling as she looked out of the window.

Mum was still brooding over Frank's situation. "I'm not sure it's a good idea to maroon him the way we did..."

"We'll go back and get him then, shall we?" Dad joked, and Cherry screamed, "No wayyyyyyyyyyy!"

We didn't return to the cabin until two days later, which was the last day of our holiday. We had a splendid time at the beaches, went to spectacular village festivals, and visited the magnificent castles. But the most memorable time was when, on our way to Gandia, Mum discovered her fear of heights. Dad had suggested an alternative scenic route, and the ride was proceeding pleasantly until we found ourselves on a long, winding road, cut into the side of a huge mountain.

"Look!" I said, captivated by the breathtaking panorama of multi-shaded forest far below.

Mum had been concentrating on her driving up

until then, but when she realized the road was nothing but a narrow shelf on the hill, without any guard rail to the right, and a sheer drop of thousands of feet below, she stopped the car at once. She sat rigid and stared ahead, her eyes wide and frightened.

"No, no, no... I can't do this," she gasped, her voice shrill and trembling.

I'd never seen Mum that way - Mum, the epitome of calmness and composure, was falling apart. There was a queue of impatient cars behind us, tooting away like a gaggle of wild geese.

Dad had to step into the driving seat.

I wasn't sure if we'd ever get home again because I'd never seen Dad drive. But, surprisingly, he took to it quickly and drove us all the way to Gandia and then back to the hotel in Xativa. From then on, he did all the driving.

We didn't know what to expect as we approached the cabins in Llocnou, but we saw at once from the make-shift compound gate that all was not as it should have been. Our clothes and other possessions were strewn like debris all over the place; my shirts and Mum's floral dress were in the swimming pool; a pair of Dad's shoes had been flung into a bush, and Cherry's I-pad dumped on the lawn. The windows and doors had been yanked off their hinges, and all the furniture inside the cabin wrecked. Not a single item had been left unscathed. The fridge was on its side, and its contents all over the floor among the smashed plates and broken bottles. The bedrooms had been similarly vandalized, and all the curtains and bed sheets ripped. But most chilling of all was the message Frank had left on the bathroom wall, written with Mum's lipstick in harsh, crooked letters:

I'M GOING BACK TO TUNBRIDGE WELLS TO TRASH YOUR HOUSE, YOU UNGRATEFUL SWINE.

Mum stared at the scene, aghast.

Dad's eyes darted from side to side, like a cornered convict with nowhere left to hide.

"Come, guys. We must leave at once. The last thing we want is for Mick to call the police and make us miss our flight."

That's if there is a home to go back to, I thought.

Cherry hadn't left the car because she didn't want to see Frank. When we returned, she didn't ask what else we'd seen.

Dad drove all the way to the airport and we were in silence while each of us, in our own stricken way, mulled over likely scenes of devastation of our lovely home. Mum still looked shell-shocked. She was thinking of her ornate china set bequeathed to her by her grand-mother. It was the only thing of value in the house - Dad reckoned it'd be worth over £6,000 if only Mum would allow him to take it to *Antiques Roadshow*. I squeezed my eyes tightly, trying to shut out the vision of our family heirloom smashed to smithereens on the kitchen floor. Dad pursed his lips, his jaw was taut and his eyes gleamed ominously.

A pall of gloom descended on us right through the flight until we landed in Gatwick, and it didn't lift when we got into the taxi that took us back home. It didn't feel as if we'd been on holiday at all. We were even more stressed than when we'd started out for the holiday a week before.

As we turned into the estate, Mr Choudary was standing outside his newsagent shop. He waved at us, but Mum and Dad didn't appear to see him. They were holding hands, their fingers intertwined in a clasp of desperate solidarity. The tension in the car was suffocating. We all breathed in short, shallow bursts and fixed our eyes firmly ahead.

But when we got to the house, we were astonished to find no evidence of damage. My legs wobbled as I followed Dad. He hesitated before unlocking the front door. We went in on tiptoes and carefully checked each room. The place was spotlessly clean as we left it. Everything was in order. Mum went straight to the kitchen. She sighed with relief, some colour returning to her face.

"Look!" shouted Cherry.

She was gazing through the drawn window curtain at the house of the Andersons across the street. Mum and Dad rushed to her side. I squeezed into the space between Cherry and Dad. The door had been smashed in, and the entire window glazing shattered. Blue and red paint had been splashed haphazardly across the exterior white walls, and the grotesque artwork was punctuated with obscenities, scrawled in menacing black letters.

"Damn!" Dad swore, and then went out to talk to one of the estate neighborhood cadets standing just outside the Andersons' vandalized house. He grunted when Dad arrived beside him.

"Looks like you missed the show," the cadet said, "Luckily, no-one was hurt."

"What happened?" Dad asked.

"Domestics," he said briefly, and then he continued when he saw Dad's inquisitive eyebrows. "Tim Anderson's long-lost brother turned up after forty years to take revenge. After smearing paint all over the walls, he smashed every piece of furniture in the house with an axe. Then he disappeared…"

"D - Disappeared?" Dad stammered.

"Yes, he went on the run. But the police caught him before he could leave the country."

"How on earth did the police find him…?" Dad asked, perplexed.

The cadet smiled indulgently at Dad. "There's nothing on any database the police can't get their hands on. And you'd be surprised what you can find out with a little bit of hacking and poking around on the internet."

A Judas in Our Midst

Reverend Bartholomew Vickers' least favourite duty was greeting his flock after the Sunday morning service. Standing by the draughty entrance of the Rentford Baptist Temple in a ridiculous white frock was bad enough, but having to smile and indulge his parishioners with meaningless chitchat as their miserable faces filed past him only added insult to injury.

"...Ah, God bless you, young man," he said in his soft, benevolent voice, patting Terry's mass of black curly hair. "One believes you'll be joining the praise and worship band very soon..." *The unkempt scallywag; the only band for him is a choir of constipated bullfrogs. That mischievous glint in his left eye; no doubt he'll wind up in jail someday.*

Reverend Vickers nodded courteously at the middle-aged couple who followed the boy. "God bless you, Tom and Jeanette. Always delighted to see you." *What a pair of leeches... Just look at them. If only their God-fearing friends knew what heinous schemes festered in their hearts!*

Tom was the church treasurer, and Jeanette helped run the Sunday school.

A pair of knackered donkeys fit only for the butcher's axe. "May the gracious Lord reward you mightily for the priceless work you have both been doing in the church..."

Next, it was Nathaniel Johnson and his anorexic wife, Amelia. *Ugh, those witch eyes! She could well have exited the church on a broomstick.* "God bless you, Mr and Mrs Johnson."

The couple had started attending the church about eight months earlier, and were now prominent members. Nathaniel helped prepare the church bulletin, and Amelia worked with Jeanette in Sunday school. They had even made their house available for Wednesday prayer meetings. Nathaniel was a grim-faced, rapidly balding man with an inscrutable personality. The vicar could only guess what he did for a living; he imagined Nathaniel might be a secondary school teacher.

"An excellent sermon today, Reverend Vickers. It was refreshing indeed!" said Nathaniel.

"Hypocrite!" the vicar yelled in his mind. The whole point of his long, sonorous rant that morning had been to shake the complacency of his congregation - especially the no-gooders, the gossipmongers, the perverts and layabouts who made up the majority. It irked him intensely that no matter what he said up there on the pulpit, no matter how much hell and damnation he spouted, his rebukes were always returned with the

same fawning, smiling faces.

"The sermon is always inspired by His grace," the vicar sighed with stretched humility. "It's such a pleasure to be the Father's messenger."

Old Gracie Fothergill followed the Johnsons, because Amelia looked after her and took her back home from church.

"May the blessing and peace of God be with you," the vicar intoned, taking Gracie's tiny fingers in his own firm, hairy hand.

She was in her late eighties, fragile as a tarantula. Wisps of pure white hair peeped from underneath the multi-coloured woollen teapot warmer that adorned her wrinkled head. Her thick-lensed, black plastic-rimmed spectacles hideously magnified her watery eyes.

"Can't wait to see you again next Sunday," she croaked.

The vicar flinched inwardly.

"By the grace of God," he smiled and withdrew his hand so swiftly he could well have been holding the claw of a vulture. "Be seeing you again next Sunday, for sure," he added, though he desperately hoped she'd have passed on before that day, relieving the world of her skeletal shuffle and toothless smile.

And so, on and on it went until they were all gone, which took over an hour. The vicar adjusted his collar gracefully, but inwardly cursed the imbecile who had invented such a ghastly accessory. The damn thing was gradually tightening around his neck and choking the life out of him.

He made his way down the central aisle of the 400-seat chapel hall. The bright, airy interior was a classic cathedral space - high-domed ceilings impressed with stained-glass windows at the sides and front. Large paintings with biblical themes adorned the white walls. One such painting - of a lamb with a cascade of copious white fleece and a halo around its head - hung above the marble altar. It bore an inscription in Gothic calligraphy: 'Holy, Holy, Holy.'

"Christ!" lamented the vicar. *"Is this the rapture that you promised?"* His despair was profound. If he had to look into the face of another pathetic parishioner, he was bound to strangle someone. It was a miracle he'd managed to stretch it this far without snapping. Self-control. That was the sole virtue of his ministry. If anyone had it in spades, that'd be him. The art of boiling inside with rage and repulsion but never betraying his innermost thoughts - not even to his nearest and dearest. He'd always struggled to see the point of it all. Even in his holy vocation, it all boiled down to the same insecurities and concerns. Everything was shrouded in an omnipresent doom and despair that tainted what should have been his happiest moments.

His office was upstairs at the end of a long, narrow passage. The small room had a square window overlooking the street, and was bare except for a desk and an unpadded wooden chair. The only painting on the wall was one of Jesus on the cross with a crown of thorns on his head. The vicar thought it curious that, despite the depth of his suffering, his face remained placid and inscrutable. The vicar wished he could endure his own suffering with the same defiance.

He gathered his robe around him and slowly eased himself into the chair behind his desk. The only un-opened envelope lay in the middle of the desk, separate from the rest of the paperwork as if it were in quarantine. He wasn't going to open it because he knew what it contained. A letter in a similar envelope, a few days earlier, had caused him some trauma. It had been from a builder's solicitor, threatening to sue the church for non-payment for works carried out on the rear extension the previous year. There was simply not enough money in the church accounts to pay the build-er. The Reverend had already put the matter to the board, and they had discussed several options that ranged from seeking another emergency loan to - God forbid - declaring the church bankrupt.

"Why aren't you finished yet? I've been waiting in the car park for the past twenty minutes. I thought you'd be all done by now."

The vicar was startled by Rachael's stern matronal voice. "*Blast!*" he said to himself, instantly regretting this harsh and unwanted intrusion into his peaceful deliber-ation. He'd been sitting there for a while, staring at the painting, lost in thought.

"Sorry dear, just tying up a few loose ends, but I'm ready now; let's go."

He tucked the unopened envelope under the pile of paperwork, picked up his leather-bound Bible, locked the office door, and followed his wife out of the church.

Rachael was no ordinary vicar's wife. She took her role very seriously and rallied the women around the events of the church like a mother hen. She also took the sermon when the vicar was away ministering at other churches. Otherwise, during the services, she was normally in the back room, organizing the tea and biscuits or performing other essential behind-the-scenes duties. Her father was a vicar, and she'd learned all the tricks of the trade from her mother.

"We'll be stopping at the Metro to pick up some groceries," she chimed as she got behind the wheel of their old blue Renault 11. The vicar got into the front passenger seat and closed the door, taking special care with his robe.

"Did you remember to make the announcement about the summer retreat?" Rachel asked, then continued without waiting for a reply, as was her habit, "Well still, it's several months away, isn't it? So, how did the sermon go down this morning? Of course, the church always appreciates your superb teachings; we're all so blessed to have you as our pastor, darling..." Rachel was in full flight now.

"Did I say I'll be going to Mum and Dad's tomorrow evening...? I'll have your other robe mended first, of course ..."

Rachael talked constantly.

She leapt from one subject to another like a vervet monkey in a caravan park full of mango trees. The vicar often wondered how she'd managed to drive so far without crashing into another vehicle or running over a pedestrian.

"...I honestly do wonder how long we have to wait for our prayer to be answered... I do long to be a mum too. Attending to those lovely children in the Sunday school, that doesn't make it easy at all... Sometimes I feel like Hannah in the Bible. Don't get me wrong, I know that God's time is the best, as you always say... After all, Hannah finally gave birth to Samuel at the ripe old age of 90. Although I'm 46 already, I wouldn't like to wait that long, even if it is still possible to become pregnant at that age..."

The vicar remained silent.

"...Yes, I know that God moves in mysterious ways, and all that," she went on, "but on this one matter, I think it is about time He started moving in the right direction, don't you agree?"

She crunched the gears and turned into the side street that led to the Tesco Express. "...Have you seen Tom and Jeanette's new car? For a couple of retired schoolteachers, you wonder where they get the money! If we should ever buy a car like that, I'd like it to be dark blue, not red like theirs. I think theirs is far too showy. That ghastly woman, Amelia... I absolutely can't stand the way she talks down to people. She led the prayer group last Thursday. Ugh! It was awful... Frankly, I don't know who she thinks she is..."

Finally, they reached their house on Beacon Hill, on the other side of Renford, and the vicar sighed as he stepped out of the car.

"... Don't you think we ought to get Thomas to

check this car tomorrow? I don't like the way it's screeching when I turn the steering wheel to the left. It's on its last legs, that's for sure. I wonder when we'll finally be able to get a new car..."

Around 6 pm the next day, which was Monday, Nathaniel rushed to the vicar's house. The vicar's wife had called, and Amelia had picked up the phone. She'd had to go up to the bedroom to fetch Nathaniel. "I don't like the way she's always asking to speak to you, without saying hi, she's such a snob, that woman."

Nathaniel was not particularly endeared to the vicar's wife, either. He felt she was too overbearing. Truth be told, he was sorry for poor Reverend Vickers, who had to put up with her for the rest of his life. Nathaniel couldn't stand her company for two seconds. "I wonder what she's calling about this time."

The conversation ran for more than fifteen minutes. It started with "Hello Nat, just a quick word about the format of the new church bulletin..." It proceeded to the important matter of the church's donation to overseas charities, which Nathaniel had been appointed to organize. That was followed by a brief lecture on how to care for the Sansevieria, which Nathaniel was later to learn was a potted houseplant. And then she finally came to the reason why she had called. Her voice suddenly turned urgent, but it was not panicked. "Could you possibly pop in and see the vicar immediately? I don't know who else to call about this situation. He'll tell you himself what it's about as soon as you get here."

Nathaniel would have given some excuse and backed out of the errand, but something in her voice stopped him.

As he pulled up on the roadside in front of the vicar's mid-terrace town house on Beacon Hill, he wondered what matter required his presence so urgently. Perhaps he was about to be given more duties in the church. He wouldn't object to that, considering his present circumstances. He'd be happy to be fully involved right until the very end.

Rachael met Nathaniel at the door. "Thanks for coming at such short notice," she said, her eyes devoid of their usual sparkle. She looked tired and drawn, and she was clutching a Bible in her right hand. "I've been reading the Psalms to him all day. He's been sitting like a zombie since 6 am, just staring into space. He hasn't eaten anything or had his tea, and he won't say a word. I've prayed and sung to him all day, and now I've completely run out of ideas," She sighed.

"Hi, Reverend," Nathaniel greeted, lowering himself gingerly on to the edge of the settee directly opposite the vicar's figure, which appeared so devoid of life and motion that it reminded Nathaniel of Lot's wife, turned into a pillar of salt. He leaned forward and looked into the middle-aged man's vacant grey eyes. "How are you?"

Nathaniel knew what he was looking at.

As a former clinical psychologist, he'd seen enough patients with that dead look in their eyes and such an air of complete self-withdrawal. But he wasn't entirely sure whether to consider the stricken vicar as a patient or a priest. Was he expected to offer a diagnosis or pray for a miracle?

As far as he knew, no-one was aware of his profession, so perhaps as an "elder" in the church, he ought to tell the pastor that this was an attack of the Devil. His faith was being tested by no less than Lucifer himself. As a man of God, he should draw upon the presence of the Holy Spirit and engage in an intensive session of fasting and prayer.

But the vicar himself knew all that. Telling him that would be like a frog trying to teach a dog to wag its tail.

This problem with the vicar was an entirely new scenario for Nathaniel. He'd never had to attend to anyone suffering from any kind of psychosis outside his professional duties. He studied people, of course, and made judgments, but these he kept to himself. After all, he'd clearly observed signs and mannerisms amongst his fellow parishioners that indicated psychological disturbance. Take James, the organist, for instance. That perpetual fixed smile that put such a strain on his face said enough about his unstable state of mind. Then there was Jeanette, who was constantly fiddling with her handbag and given to emotional outbursts during Bible classes. Even young Terry, with his twitching eye and discordant, almost hysterical voice in the church choir, was clearly teetering on the edge of a mental crisis.

But in the church, it was all under the control of the Holy Spirit. The vicar himself was always warning and admonishing in his sermons that the Devil was ready to pounce in the most devious ways and should be resisted at all times with fervent prayers and reading of the Holy Bible. The vicar's wife dedicated many of her sermons to the banishment of demons and evil spirits that sought to interfere with the happiness of God's children. There was no room for poverty, sin, depression or any of the attacks of the evil one.

Rachael had disappeared into the kitchen for about ten minutes. She reappeared with a small tray of tea and biscuits, and hovered at the doorway as she looked anxiously at Nathaniel.

"Has he said anything?"

"I'm sorry, he hasn't, Mrs Vickers. I don't know how to say this, but I think your husband is suffering from depression, and I'd certainly recommend that he makes an appointment at St Peter's Hospital as soon as possible."

Rachael placed the tray carefully and slowly on the small stool beside the settee. She had paled visibly, and her eyes were cold and hard as she stared at Nathaniel. He immediately realized he'd said the wrong thing. He'd misfired. He'd uttered a terrible blasphemy.

"How dare you speak like that about the vicar!" she spat at him. "Who the hell do you think you are - a bloody psychologist?" She took in a refreshing lungful of air and appeared to calm down for a second. But she continued, "I've never heard such nonsense in my life. Now, please leave this house at once!"

Nathaniel set off back home in a daze but gradually recovered. His mumbled apologies hadn't saved him from being kicked out by the vicar's wife. He reckoned she would come round and would soon realize she'd overreacted. The vicar himself wouldn't remain in his stupor for long. He'd soon snap out of it. But the episode would recur, and if left unattended might turn into a bigger problem of prolonged melancholy.

By the time Nathaniel reached home, he'd shrugged off his mixed feelings about Rachael's outburst. After all, he had his own problems to deal with.

The following Sunday, the vicar was not in church. He'd been invited to preach at The Apostles' Lodge, a sister church in North London.

Nathaniel and Amelia arrived at the church a few minutes late because they had to pick up Gracie on the way. The old woman was becoming increasingly frail, and it took longer to get her prepared and helped into the back seat of their Rover. Amelia was determined they'd do everything to get the octogenarian to the church, as long as it was Gracie's desire.

As Amelia was not on Sunday school duty that day, she helped Nathaniel get Gracie to the place they normally sat, four benches from the front. But the seats were already taken, so they had to drag their way to the front bench, which everyone always avoided.

When Nathaniel discovered who was conducting the sermon, he winced. He never enjoyed Rachael's preaching. It was always delivered in the same spluttering tone as her one-sided conversations, without substance, and full of nonsense and contradictions.

Nathaniel had thought no further about the incident at the vicar's house. He'd even managed to avoid telling Amelia what had transpired that evening. Although neither the vicar nor his wife had called him, he was aware that the Reverend had recovered and had resumed his normal duties.

He shifted uncomfortably on the solid mahogany pew when he realized that the vicar's wife was glaring coldly at him from the pulpit. It was obvious that all had not been forgiven. Even then, he didn't imagine she'd do anything rash.

"Brethren," she declared, "we have a Judas in our midst!"

A hush fell over the congregation, and some parishioners shifted uneasily in their pews, their eyes downcast. Then she said it again.

"Yes, brethren, we have a *Judas* amongst us."

Silence reigned supreme as all eyes swivelled towards Nathaniel.

"In these pews today sits a traitor who has been partaking of the holy bread before the altar and has been spreading awful rumours about our vicar. Among us today, a serpent in the Garden of Eden... A scorpion with a lethal sting in its tail... By their fruits, ye shall know them!"

There was no mistaking whom she was talking about. The vicar's wife's finger, now trembling, was pointing at Nathaniel, who remained frozen on his seat. He felt a rush of blood to his head, and his mouth instantly dried up. He heard Amelia's sharp breath and from the corner of his eye saw that she'd stood up. Amelia stomped out of the church with all the dignity her slender frame could muster. Even old Gracie stood up with an agility that took Nathaniel by surprise, and muttered incoherently as she left in a hurry. Nathaniel did not leave with his head bowed. He surveyed the sea of bemused faces. Although he hadn't always been a serious Christian, he'd never walked out of the church during a sermon. He certainly didn't want to cause a scene in the church. For now, it was best to leave as quietly as possible and rejoin Amelia and Grace. In any case, that would be the last time he'd be setting foot in a church.

The next Sunday's service was conducted by the vicar. He was taken aback by the size of the congregation. The whole place was packed to the joists. The front pews were filled with the most unlikely characters; hardly the type you'd expect to find within the walls of a church. Others stood at the back and in the wings throughout the service. Reverend Vickers was aware of what had transpired in church the previous Sunday, and he'd had strong words with his wife. He'd also tried unsuccessfully to contact Nathaniel and Amelia and offer his sincere apologies. But they weren't answering their phone, and when he went to their house, no-one was there. Now, he scanned the congregation for any sign of them, but neither of them was there. Not even old Gracie, who had never missed a service since he'd assumed his vicarage of the parish.

That aside, the vicar was pleased with the turnout that day. The collection would boost the church's meagre funds. And fortunately, he'd prepared an upbeat sermon packed with some decent jokes he'd got off the internet. The vicar knew the previous Sunday's drama in the church was the main reason for the large turnout. Rumours had spread like wildfire throughout Rentford and the surrounding districts that a drama was unfolding at the Rentford Baptist Temple. They'd all turned up for the entertainment, to witness the public flaying of prominent church members. It was the circus come to town again; a Pentecostal version of Jerry Springer's TV show. But the vicar failed to meet the congregation's expectations, and his sermon, rather than fanning the flames of local gossip, in fact put half of the congregation to sleep.

The greeting of the flock after the service was most excruciating for the vicar. He shook hands with every one of the new attendants, and extracted their unfailing promise that they'd come again the next Sunday.

Although he was exhausted, he felt his spirit lighten considerably as his wife drove them back home in their beleaguered blue Renault 11. Also, in an astonishing act of divine intervention, Rachael remained silent through-out the drive.

The vicar's euphoria was short-lived. He'd meant to take a quick nap after lunch and then prepare a note for the evening prayer meeting, but he found himself unable to work up the appetite to tackle the roast potato and beef that stared back complacently from his plate.

He was alarmed by the frequent episodes of lethargy he'd been experiencing in recent months. Sometimes, when he picked up his Bible and read a psalm or a chapter from his favourite Book of Corinthians, it actually did cheer him up. But there were times when he didn't have the energy or willpower even to pick up the Bible.

Rachael was in and out of the living room, busy with her endless chores. She stopped and then went and sat with him at the round dining table.

"Are you alright, Bart?"

"Certainly," he sighed and said, "God's grace is sufficient."

She held her husband's hand and looked into his eyes. She wanted to say something, but she stopped herself, leaving it for him to read the worry and concern on her face.

The following week was the worst time of their lives. The vicar stayed in bed most days, drifting in and out of his melancholy, and Rachael ran around trying to fill in for his missed engagements and attend to his needs. She read the Bible to him and played a CD of his favourite Graham Kendrick praise and worship songs. She was sure this period of his trial would soon pass, and the good vicar would be restored to a greater glory. In the meantime, she was determined to hold the fort, and do whatever had to be done.

"Rachael," he said on Saturday morning, during a brief reprieve from his suffering, "I've never told you enough how much I love you. I know you've been working terribly hard taking care of me, and I just want to say thank you. But we have to tell the church that I can't possibly carry on. I'm so ill with this thing..."

"God forbid it, Bart!" she exclaimed sharply. "As a man of God, you can't just stand in front of the congregation and tell them you're suffering from depression, and want to pack it in. That's the same as declaring that Satan has won the battle!"

"I'm sorry, Rachael, I've thought long and prayed hard about it, and I've made up my mind. God willing, I will make an announcement to the Church tomorrow, and we'll arrange for a stand-in vicar..."

"No, no, no!" Rachael would hear no more of it. She fled the bedroom in an uncontrolled fit of sobbing and no small measure of rage.

Reverend Vickers could not attend the service on Sunday. Not because he was down with depression, but because someone had left an urgent message on his voice mail. It was all garbled, and he had to replay it several times to make any sense of it. It seemed one of his parishioners was in the hospital. He abandoned the idea of calling the hospital again after thirty minutes waiting for someone to pick up the phone. The only option left was to go out there.

"The Spirit tells me it could be old Gracie," he said to his wife.

"Yes, she's been quite poorly, and she's not as nimble as she used to be. I do hope she pulls through this time."

That made it all the more urgent, because the vicar was aware that the old woman had no known relatives. He, as her vicar, was all that she had, and if she was on her death-bed, then he'd have to be by her side as a matter of duty.

Reverend Vickers had slept very badly because of the announcement he was planning to make. Moreover, Rachael was utterly disconsolate, and she hadn't stopped weeping all night. It was painful to see how red her eyes had become and how puffy her face was from crying.

He'd almost considered not going to the church after all, but he managed to eke out enough energy to get out of bed and follow up on his resolve. But now the phone message somehow deflected his thoughts from himself, and he found it easy to get ready and go to the hospital.

Seeing her husband's new-found motivation, Rachael was clearly relieved, and it was astonishing how quickly the puffiness disappeared, and she suddenly brightened up.

"Don't you worry about me, dear," said the vicar. "I'll take a cab to see Grace at the hospital. Please go ahead with the church duties this morning. Don't tell them anything just yet. If it's possible, I'll join you during the service."

"Of course. I pray Gracie gets better."

As the vicar approached the hospital, his nerves tingled with apprehension. It suddenly occurred to him that he'd never performed the last rites. Christenings and weddings were a doddle. Even funerals were fine. It was surprising how one could conduct them with such detachment. But to look a dying person in the eye and say the words to comfort and guide her on her final journey was something he'd never done, and it filled him with an overwhelming dread. He closed his eyes briefly and muttered a prayer of reassurance. Then he stepped up to the main reception desk and asked where he could find the patient he'd been called to see.

The vicar's belief in his own intuition took a knock when he discovered it wasn't old Gracie who was in the hospital; it was Nathaniel Johnson. And he was in the cancer ward. As the vicar entered the ward, he saw Nathaniel's prostrate figure on the hydraulic bed. Next to him was Amelia, who stood up as the vicar entered. Nathaniel was emaciated and his face was pale. His eyes were deep hollows in his head, and the blue veins on his left temple seemed to be shuddering between pulses. He smiled lamely, and his eyes followed the vicar's progress as he made his way to his bedside, then gently covered Nathaniel's hand.

Amelia's eyes were red, but her face was composed and somewhat defiant. Instinctively, all three knew that for Nathaniel, this clearly was the end.

Nathaniel's voice was barely a whisper, but the glistering white walls of the small room amplified its resonance, rendering it as a crisp rasp.

"It's okay, Reverend Vickers. Amelia and I have known about this for more than nine months. That's why I quit my practice and started attending church more. I was brought up in a Christian household, but I drifted away and lost my faith. We started going back to church so that at this final moment a godly person like you could be by my side to usher me on my way to paradise where I will be amidst loved ones who have passed on before... I've paid my meagre pittance of faith, and I hold fast to the belief in God's promise. The promise that neutralizes the fear of death..."

His eyes roved languidly in the direction of his wife, and a vague smile flittered across his sallow face. She leaned forward and held his other hand.

Even at that instant, despite the gravity of the occasion, the vicar was cheered by the reflection that it wasn't as awful or as morbid as he'd expected. Nathaniel was not overwhelmed by remorse, and Amelia was not stricken with grief. More importantly, the whole place was not overflowing with gloom. Rather, it was graceful and serene. *"O death, where is thy sting?"* was the scoffing refrain that danced about in the vicar's head. He held the hand of the dying man, his own mind totally free of its usual burden of bitterness and remorse. It was as if life was passing from the limp, withered hand into his own faltering being.

"His grace is sufficient," the vicar reassured Nathaniel and his wife. Then he proceeded to read some verses from John 14 in his Bible.

Nathaniel's face sagged, and a sharp rush of breath escaped from his parted lips. His eyes remained open, but the spark had gone out of them.

Over the weeks that followed, the vicar became

more occupied with the works of his calling. Since the experience by Nathaniel's death-bed, the bouts of gloom had practically disappeared. He didn't declare it a miracle. All he knew was that as long as he engaged his thoughts with the welfare of others, rather than dwell constantly on his own concerns, he felt all the better for it.

The New Village Teacher

"Silence!" Mr Stephens pounded his fist on the dilapidated and dusty teacher's desk.

The noise and commotion didn't stop immediately, not until all of us realized that the principal had brought a guest with him. It was the first time I'd ever seen a person in a suit and tie except in newspapers, magazines and text books. I noticed that the visitor's suit was dark blue, and his shirt was blazing white. His tie had shiny, mesmerizing stripes that were red, blue and green, almost like the plumage of the wild ducks in the Moloko pond. Standing next to him in three-quarter length khaki shorts and brown leather sandals, Mr Stephens looked like an underpaid district guard escorting a bank manager around and hoping for a decent tip.

We wondered who this stranger was. Maybe he was an inspector, or a government official from the Federal

Ministry of Education. Judging from his attire and deportment, he'd have to be a high-ranking superintendent, probably the Commissioner himself. We wondered why he had come to our school.

"Listen, you students!" Mr Stephens announced. "Mr Oriola is your new teacher."

A shuddering gasp of disbelief ran through the entire class, followed by a brief moment of stunned silence. Then normal pandemonium was resumed.

After Mr Stephens left, the new teacher stood in front of us. He didn't say anything. He just stood there smiling a somewhat benevolent smile until the noise-making abated. Some of the students were there only because it was the first day of term. They were usually the ones who quickly got bored and became noisy and disruptive in class. But now, even they had fallen silent out of curiosity.

"I want you all to join me in a little preliminary exercise." This teacher had a deep silky voice and a polished accent that caused everyone to sit up and pay attention, at least for a bit. "I need two volunteers, please."

When nobody answered, he pointed to Sule Abims, the tallest boy in the class. Then he pointed to me.

"Yes, you," he said, "the bespectacled young fellow."

They were not real glasses. They were just an old frame without any lenses that I'd found on the waste tip on my way to Grandpa's cassava farm. I wore them because I thought they made me look intelligent.

"I want both of you to cover this blackboard with these strips." He opened his black leather briefcase and took out a pack of white cardboard strips, each measuring about 12 inches wide and 18 inches in length. Peeling off bits of tape at the ends of each strip, we found they were sticky and would bond with the blackboard, despite the chalk and dust that coated its surface. In a bit, the class was staring at an entirely covered blackboard.

Once again, he opened his briefcase and took out what looked like a small digital camera. He placed it on the broken, dust-coated desk and switched it on. Nothing happened immediately except for a tiny red light that flashed steadily at the corner of the device.

Then he turned to the class. "Okay, my dear ladies and gentlemen, as you can see, we have turned our blackboard here into a whiteboard!"

A few of the students thought it was some kind of joke and began to laugh, but they quickly shut up when the whole class did not join them.

The new teacher put a notebook on the table beside the camera-like appliance, scribbled at the top of an open page, and drew a small star on the paper. As he did, the writing appeared on the whiteboard, etched in an intense purple streak.

"Albert Oriola. That's my name, and the star is my sign. I want you to come forward one by one, in an orderly fashion of course, and write your name down clearly in your best possible handwriting, and draw your symbol. Please don't use my symbol or anybody else's. You need your own."

Eze was the first. He was one of those serious students whose notes others often borrowed after classes to copy into their own notebooks. He wrote his name boldly underneath the teacher's, followed by a box with a cross inside. The other pupils took their turn, and soon the class had filled the whole board with their names and symbols. Some were simple shapes: a circle, triangle, square, etc; others were more complex ones: a hoe, a double-sided cutlass, a musket, several types of knives and guns. I opted for a crude sketch of a Honda 175 motorbike.

By the time we were done, it was almost time for afternoon break.

"That'll be all for today. With introductions safely out of the way, I look forward to seeing you all here tomorrow when we will begin, in earnest, with a bit of mathematics."

Normally, any mention of maths guaranteed that the class would be almost empty the following day. But, somehow, I guessed every one of us would be present this time.

I couldn't wait to tell Gramps all about our new teacher, but when I got home that day, Baba Jegede was there. Although Jegs - as he preferred us to call him - was not quite as old as Gramps, he was my grandfather's best mate.

"He only arrived from England a few months ago," Jegs was telling Gramps. "Jerome says his farewell party in London was broadcast on radio, on TV and... and... on the Satellite Navigation System! Imagine that!"

Jerome was Jegs' son, who lived in the US. He always kept Jegs updated on current world affairs, so his father never missed a story.

"...he received many awards for his outstanding achievements in science, and technology and... and... 'Enjimatics'..."

Gramps gawked in unabashed admiration as Jegs rattled on with more details about my new teacher.

"But when he arrived at Alawada Airport, there was no-one to welcome him back to his homeland. Not a single government official or ministry representative or any newspaper people... or... pe... pe... 'pepperoni'! (By which I was to realize, at a future time, that he meant 'paparazzi'.) He and his wife had to make their way to Karago in an old, rickety mammy wagon."

"Hmm...That's such a shame," Gramps commiserated, wagging his head. "You'd at least expect such an important person would get a bit of recognition in his own country."

"Of course..." Jegs agreed, and then lowered his voice to a conspiratorial whisper. "That man sent 20 thousand pounds to his brothers to have their father's old house - his family home - refurbished. But then they blew all the money on palm wine and bean cakes. Not a penny went to fixing the ruin, which had become the home for the goats and agama lizards." Jegs wrinkled his nose and waved his hand as if to ward off offending odour. "The place was in quite a state when Albert and his wife moved in."

Gramps' mouth fell open. "What! You mean the newly-arrived man and his wife are now living in that wretched place?"

"His wife already had enough. She packed up all her *jagbajantis* and fled back to her children in the UK."

"Who'd blame her, eh? Who'd blame her?" muttered Gramps. "I'm sure the man will follow soon. It's only a matter of time."

"I'm not so sure about that, Papa Daramola. He's been pretty rugged so far. Did you know he offered to work with the government? Advise them on matters of education, health and... and 'ecomatics'. They didn't want anything to do with him. They told him to take his 'ecomatics' and ... and..." Jegs let his words trail off, and then, recovering, he continued, "You know what they called him?"

"What?"

"Professor Jantis!"

Gramps shook his head, as if that would clear his brain of the incredulity of the whole thing.

Baba Jegede continued. "What does he have to offer, anyway, eh? Does he think we do our ecomatics here in Banania the same way they do ecomatics overseas?"

I waited at the door, listening to Jegs. I often wondered where he'd lived before he came and settled in our village.

"He even wanted to teach in some of the universities, but no-one would let him. They didn't want him to confuse our own professors with his ecomatics."

"That's a great shame. They'd have benefited from his wealth of knowledge, I expect," Gramps said.

"Of course!" Jegs agreed. "But that's not all of it. Here in the village, he went to the elders and councillors with his ideas about water, electricity, health centres and all that... they told him to... just get on his cockroach horse and gallop away into the land of the dancing elves. Who does he think he is, trying to teach them how to spend the district budget? Why should they let some ignorant overseas-trained professor use his... his... crooked ecomatics to deny them their individual share of government money?"

Jegs chuckled.

Gramps took out his battered tin snuff box and snorted a pinch of tobacco.

"Anyway," Jegs went on, "they all know that the most important thing to do is to set aside enough money for the annual visit of the Regional Superintendent."

Suddenly Jegs took notice of me.

"Sorry, young man. Your school is the only place left for our British professor to practise his ecomatics. At least there he can't do any damage. The only ones to suffer will be you poor brats who will have to endure it until he finally shuffles back to his family in England."

The next day, in maths, the teacher called out each of the students in the class. We were astonished that he knew every single student by name.

"Ayo Daramola!" Mr Oriola called out, startling me out of my enchanting daydream. "From now on, your name is Pythagoras."

An unrestrained giggle erupted from somewhere at the back of the class. Someone obviously thought "Pythagoras" was a term of ridicule. "Ignoramus" would have prompted a similar response in more enlightened circles. The rest of the class didn't know what it meant either, but they thought it definitely sounded like a dreadful insult. They were glad that the insult hadn't been fired in their direction, and I was dismayed that I'd be the butt of many jokes for days to come.

"You, Pythagoras of Samos, are the great, ancient philosopher and mathematician who invented the most significant formula in geometry. You propounded many useful theories, and you brought about a clearer understanding of nature. The whole world owes you an enormous debt." He bowed in my direction and clapped, and the rest of the class joined in, startling me.

That day, every student in the class got a new name, and they were similarly lauded and applauded. Eze was given Isaac Newton. My friend Kayode, who was considered to be slow and often lacking in gumption, became Michael Faraday. His sister Dorcas, who was also in our class, became Marie Curie. Sule Abims became Thomas Edison. We all knew from our year 1 science that this was the man who invented electricity. Sule grinned pretentiously like an elder who had just been appointed the grand totem-bearer for our village.

The village was awash with rumours swirling around the person of Mr Oriola. He lived in his father's old house at the outskirts of the village, where no-one visited, not even his brothers. He refused to pay homage to the Grand Elder and was generally shunned by all the local chiefs. He was even out of favour with the Catechist because he'd refused to attend the village church fund-raising event.

Tongues were wagging over his eccentric behaviour. Weird noises were heard from his house and strange glows were seen emanating from his rooftop late in the night. In the daytime, when cats and dogs strayed too close to his house, they went berserk and ran away.

All the rumours invariably crystallized into the inescapable conclusion that Mr Oriola was dabbling in black magic. The whole house, they believed, was buzzing with ghosts and demons who carried out this teacher's biddings and attended to his every whim. Otherwise, how did he manage to keep his clothes so pristine? Who fetched his water and cooked his food? How did he get those shoes to glisten all the time like the twinkle in the devil's eye?

Obi, Kayode and I often argued among ourselves for hours about the whole situation. Then one day we decided to investigate. We skipped Thursday afternoon assembly and set out for Mr Oriola's house, fully assured that he was going to remain on the school premises.

The windows and doors of his bungalow had recently been replaced. The surrounding hedges were immaculate, and the back garden was in a better state than any garden I'd ever seen, despite the scattered dry leaves baked to crinkled flakes by the heat of the sun. There was an orange tree at the centre and two mango trees a bit further from the house.

The back door was ajar, and we tiptoed into the kitchen. The interior was well lit by a resplendent set of wall-mounted fixtures close to the tiled ceiling. In the city, some houses had diesel-powered generators that made a lot of noise and billowed constant plumes of nasty, foul-smelling smoke into the air. The new teacher's house obviously had electricity, but the generator was nowhere to be seen, heard or smelt. The walls were painted white, and the wooden floor was smooth and dust-free. There was a strange but pleasant smell throughout. In the sitting room, we saw a brown, soft, leather-bound lounge sofa and a centre stool that appeared to be some kind of polished white rock. The bedroom was the tidiest, indeed the most beautiful, bedroom I'd ever seen. The walls were also white, and the floor was covered with a plastic carpet patterned in black and white squares.

But there was no sign of the rumoured ghosts or demons.

There was another door which was locked. I turned away to examine a carved wooden ornament in the corner, and I heard Kayode calling from the kitchen in a hoarse whisper. The sharpness of his voice told me something was amiss. I crossed to the kitchen in a flash.

"The door has shut. I can't open it for us to get out!"

he exclaimed.

"Step aside!" ordered Obi, emerging from a side room next to the kitchen. He was a broad-shouldered lad, normally quite sure of himself. But within a minute he was wearing the most dejected and uncertain expression I'd ever seen, as it dawned on all of us that the door had no handle or keyhole. The front door was exactly the same design, as were all the windows. They also had no handles or latches.

We were trapped in the teacher's house.

My stomach churned like the grain thresher in the district plantation farm. Kayode began to sob. His father was an ex-soldier, reputed for his love of discipline. He'd take a dim view of anyone who'd break into another person's property, and if the perpetrator happened to be his own son, then the poor fellow was bound to pay the grimmest price. Obi and I were not quite as unlucky. Although our guardians had equally high expectations about our good conduct, they did not have the same appetite for meting out brutal punishment.

"Hey," I said, "I've got an idea."

Kayode's glistening eyes lit up with a glimmer of uncertain hope.

"Let's hide in the hallway. The moment he opens the door, we'll jump him and then run like hell."

From Obi's still-frightened expression, I could tell he didn't think that idea would work.

We waited in the sitting room. It was so quiet we could hear all the sounds from outside. There was a constant rustling as goats scampered about on the dry leaves under the trees. There was a random cracking of breaking twigs as rodents rampaged in the undergrowth. A male pigeon commenced cooing his romantic appeal to a reluctant female, his entreaties becoming more desperate and erratic as frustration and rejection set in.

We could even hear ourselves breathing.

Obi's deep brown eyes darted from side to side like a squirrel's in a hunter's basket trap. Then suddenly he stiffened, and his eyes widened.

I heard it too. First, a low wheeze, like the forced breathing of a bull after a lengthy chase, and then much louder, like some strange, wild animal in an absolute fit of rage. It was coming from the locked room. I shivered, and my teeth clattered. The 'thing' in the room had woken up and was clamouring for its dinner, and we were still there in the house. Again we looked around, desperately for a way out.

So, rumours of evil ghosts and demons were true, after all. Now we knew, but we'd never live to tell the tale.

"Hey, boys! What are you doing in my house?"
None of us had heard the teacher come in through the back door. We were huddled in the corner of the living room, staring with fearful, pleading eyes at the locked door, from behind which the strange sounds kept coming. The teacher ignored our pleading eyes and went straight ahead and unlocked the door. I expected a two-

headed dragon with long crooked horns and sharp teeth to leap out and rip us to shreds. But nothing happened. Instead, more light spilled out of the room and, as our eyes adjusted, we saw that the place was a sort of laboratory filled with all sorts of curious contraptions. The 'thing' making the noise was a huge, frothing barrel mounted on a metal frame. It spun and twisted vigorously, making the racket we'd heard.

"That's my washing machine," explained the teacher, smiling. Then he chuckled as he saw our faces. It must have been hilarious indeed for him to see our panic so quickly turning to relief.

I was the first to recover. "We're terribly sorry, sir. We didn't come here to steal. We were just curious."

He sighed and then shrugged. "You fellows must learn to respect other people. Respect is not just about saying "Yes sir." It is also having consideration for the possessions, property and privacy of others."

We put on our most sober and contrite expressions. Kayode even crouched and bowed his head for maximum effect.

"We're sorry, sir," we apologized in chorus.

"Okay, I'll make a deal with you. If you score over 70 in the maths test next Monday, I will forget all about this silly incident. If not, I'll report it to Mr Stephens who, I can assure you, will ensure that you are all duly and properly disciplined. Fair?"

"Thank you, sir," we chorused again, although none of us was confident about our maths. In prior tests, I'd consistently flunked outright.

"Now run along. Go back to your homes," the teacher ordered. "Don't forget about the math test on Monday!"

Mr Oriola gave each student a piece of paper. "I've taken the liberty of producing a brief biography and résumé - a list of your various and numerous outstanding achievements. Read and discuss them among yourselves. Special credit will go to anyone who finds additional information that is especially interesting.

An excited babble ensued as we eagerly compared papers.

"Wait, students... At some point, each of you will be invited to enlighten us all about your particular area of excellence. We'll then hold a contest to decide who is the greatest among you all. Who is it going to be? Marie Curie? Albert Einstein? Pythagoras?"

One of the girls, now called Ada Lovelace, raised her hand. "But sir, why is it that, among all these names of famous inventors and scientists, there isn't a single name from our country, Banania - not even one from Africa?"

A unanimous murmur of agreement rippled through the class. Then there was silence while they waited for the teacher's reply.

He smiled. But it was not his usual happy smile. "That's a jolly good question, Jumoke. It's not to say that Africans have not contributed to science, or that there have been no great Africans. There are just not many of them in recorded history, especially around the times of those whose names you now bear." He sighed, "You can become famous scientists too, despite the reluctance of your councillors and your politicians who will not give you a chance.

I have no doubt that an outstanding engineer, or an exemplary doctor, or an illustrious scholar, or a visionary leader could be sitting here right now." He switched on his usual smile again. "Perhaps, Ada, you could be that great leader. Maybe you ought to ask your politicians and your government officials why they believe none of you deserve that opportunity."

Six months after Mr Oriola first arrived at the school, he was spotted walking up the main road that led from the school gate to the old assembly hall. He was not wearing his normal suit and tie. Instead, he wore the same clothes worn by the moon men on page 17 of our science book. However, his were old, stained and crumpled. It was very much out of character for him to look so unkempt. As he came into view, we noticed he was carrying a large bucket filled with mysterious white liquid and had an enormous jute bag slung over his other shoulder.

Everyone watched him briskly make his way up the road. When he reached the old assembly building, he took out a brush and began painting the walls with the white stuff. Obi and I went up and offered to give him a hand.

"Thanks, gentlemen." He smiled and produced more brushes from the sack. "I made the paint out of finely ground dry maize and a special fixing ingredient that gives it the gloss. It's the same admixture I used to paint my house."

Before long, we were joined by more students, and later by some of the teachers. We made several trips to the teacher's house for more of the seemingly endless supply of this substance and, by sundown, all the school buildings shone in white. It was astonishing how much difference it made. The school had a resplendent look, and when the hedges were trimmed and the roads lined on both sides with large, painted boulders, the whole place truly came alive. In the weeks that followed, other houses in the village were painted too, after we learned how to tweak Mr Oriola's original recipe to get shades of purple, green, yellow and other colours.

On another day, after teaching the junior classes about water treatment and supply, Mr Oriola unveiled his latest invention. It was a large steel tank installed beside the community stream behind the school compound. No-one knew how he'd managed to get the tank there and set up the hand-wound pump and the pipes that conveyed water to the tank.

"This water filter treatment reservoir is filled with sand - several layers of coarse and fine sand," he explained to all of us bemused students. We watched as water spurted out from a bank of taps at the base of the tank.

At first, most of the villagers refused to use the filter. The teacher was summoned by the Grand Elder and made to explain why he'd installed such an abomination by the sacred stream. The chiefs asked who gave him permission and insisted that he'd displeased the gods. But when they found the water in the filter to be free of the tiny dancing insects that were widely believed to cause yellow fever, the filtered water soon became popular.

On yet another occasion, the new teacher got some students to line the school paths with poles, atop which he installed special electric globes that automatically came on at nightfall. The whole village marvelled at his ingenious use of what they called "black magic". It had to be black magic; otherwise how did this 'thing' work when there was no generator, no batteries and no wires? Others believed that it was a miracle, and the new teacher was some sort of prophet. Forget about Cerullo or Bonnké, this guy was the real deal. Some even, it was rumoured, had been miraculously cured of AIDS and other incurables, just by drinking water from his filter tank or by touching one of his lamp posts while it glowed.

"No, dear students, it's not black magic at all," he explained to the class. "You need to stop relying on black magic as the explanation for every phenomenon. Black magic is not real. The only people who benefit from black magic are those who deceive you with fake miracles. This is not a miracle. It's science. If you take your studies seriously, you'll learn how it all works, and you'll be able to put your knowledge to practical use."

That was the same day Mr Oriola distributed some papers to all students to give to their parents and guardians.

"Yes," he said, "I know that they can't read, but I am relying on you to read it to them."

As usual, Baba Jegede was with Grandpa when I arrived home with the note from the teacher. I quickly pocketed the folded piece of paper so Jegs wouldn't see it, since he was always criticizing my reading and pointing out mistakes every time I attempted to read a letter to Grandpa. Too late - he'd spotted the paper.

"Come on, read it to us," he demanded, once I'd explained where the note came from.

Grandpa's wiry brows arched expectantly, and Baba crossed his legs, rearranging his copious robe. I cleared my throat like a dignitary ready to make a momentous speech.

"You are cordially invited to the general community meeting in the newly-refurbished hall of the Missionary Secondary School. We will discuss various ideas about improving our community. We will talk about water supply, electricity, the communal clinic, our schools and more. We will talk about what we can do to make our village better for us and for our children. I trust you will attend, and I look forward to your contribution to this worthwhile event. The meeting will take place on 14 October 1983, at 4:30 pm.

"Hmmm..." Baba Jegede stroked his patchy beard. For once he hadn't stopped me during a reading. I felt pleased, although I couldn't help but notice the frown that had suddenly clouded his rugged face. "But that is the same day as the Regional Councillor's visit, isn't it? Not a single person will be at that meeting. Everyone will be busy attending to His Excellency."

"True," Grandpa agreed. "Everyone's been preparing for the Councillor's visit. Haruna and his apprentices are tapping the palm wine and filling the gourds as we speak. The cows have already been purchased; fat cows they are, lounging unwary in the Elders' yard, awaiting the slaughterer's knife. And the women... they have been practising the traditional welcome dance. Have you seen the town hall? It's been swept and decorated. Maybe it will even be painted to make it more presentable..."

I'd forgotten all about the annual visit of the Regional Councillor. It was the most festive time in the village, a time I always looked forward to. I'd been involved in the acrobatic performance which we did on that day, and I'd collected new buttons to sew into my *Egungun* costume. But now I had misgivings. For all the entertainment and hospitality lavished on the Councillor, it was difficult to see what the community got back in return. Yes, the "big man" would come with his entourage, and he would be escorted through the village to the communal hall where he'd make his customary pompous speech. He'd be wined, dined, fêted and conferred with yet another honorary chieftaincy award - a real miracle it was that the village has never run out of chieftaincy titles. And then he would go away, never to be heard from or seen again until the next campaign rally.

In the days that followed, we all learned a lot from Mr Oriola. Many of those things I would never have learned from anyone else. I never had any real ideas about what lay ahead, and I rarely thought things through.

"You must always think about where you are going with your life," he once told us.

I was thirteen, and I'd never seriously thought of what I wanted to do with my life. I simply hoped that life would work out naturally. The impending end-of-term exams didn't matter at all either. I'd likely work on the farm and save up for a second-hand motorbike and then go to the city and make a living as a motorbike taxi rider.

I was utterly unprepared when the teacher asked, "Ayo Daramola! When you are older, what will your profession be?"

My reply was automatic: "A medical doctor." I couldn't explain why I'd given him that reply.

The students fell over one another in a rush of laughter, but the teacher was not laughing.

"An excellent choice!" he exclaimed. "Now, sit down and close your eyes for a moment."

Silence.

"Ayo, imagine yourself in your doctor's coat, your stethoscope hanging from your neck and your spectacles mounted intelligently on the bridge of your nose. You are sitting at your desk in your office where there are several certificates on the wall proclaiming your magnificent credentials. An elderly man is sitting in front of you, smiling. He says, 'Doctor Ayo, I cannot thank you enough for saving the life of my only son.' Everybody in town is praising you for the work you're doing, saving lives and restoring health. Congratulations, Dr Ayo Pythagoras Daramola. You are one of the greatest doctors in the world."

Several minutes after I'd opened my eyes, I was still smiling. I was indeed going to be a doctor, a great doctor.

"You all have the potential to be doctors, engineers and accountants - anything you want to be. It will take hard work, and yes, you are at a great disadvantage because of the extremely poor standards in this school. Your school is one of the worst in the country. No student from here has ever gained admission to a good university."

There was a disgruntled but agreeing murmur from the class. Then a girl raised up her hand. "My brother attended this school and he gained admission to The Faith and Glory University in the township," she asserted proudly.

The teacher nodded, and a fleeting sad expression crossed his face. He shook his head.

"Faith and Glory is not a real university," he said flatly.

A scandalized gasp swept through the entire class. Faith and Glory was one of the most popular universities in the district. It was established by the founder of the Tabernacle Pentecostal Church. Evangelism was the only thriving enterprise in the whole country, and small-time self-styled pastors were making a killing, peddling faith and feel-good succour to ignorant people who saw no other way out of their poverty and misery. The extremely successful evangelists got to establish their own universities.

"I can assure you," Mr Oriola continued, "nowhere else on this planet, apart from the Republic of Malaria, will any company or institution accept a graduate with a certificate from a university like Faith and Glory."

"Well," another student asked, "What about Aliyu Baba University?"

Mr Oriola sighed and shook his head again. "Proper universities are never named after fraudulent politicians. You must think carefully about the universities you want to attend. Don't limit your dreams to the garbage served by incompetent leaders. You have to dream yourselves out of the bottomless pit of poverty dug for you by your selfish, greedy and corrupt politicians. You must dream of going to international universities like Cambridge, Harvard and Princeton. It's as much your entitlement as the children of the politicians who are regularly packed off to study abroad at the expense of the rest of the people in the country."

Three days before the community meeting, the revolving rumour mills were at their most vigorous. The teacher was going back to the UK. His wife had finally run out of patience and demanded that if he didn't return at once, she'd have divorce papers delivered to him by FedEx.

The preparations for the Councillor's visit were also in top gear. The chiefs joked about Mr Oriola's meeting in their gatherings, and the Elders had a hearty long laugh at our teacher's expense. Who did he think he was to be convening a community meeting without first consulting them, and - of all days - on the same day as the Regional Councillor's visit?

As for others, they'd all received Mr Oriola's invitation. Some thought the purpose was sound and the course was just. It was for the good of the village. Some even tried to get the teacher to change the date of the meeting, saying they'd be sure to attend if he changed it. After all, the welcome gathering was going to be grander, and there'd be food and drink at the welcome fête, and he wasn't going to provide any refreshments at his meeting.

"It's okay," he replied. "Of course, I'll be hugely disappointed if no-one attends, but that won't be the end of the world. It'll only tell me obviously where your priorities lie and make it easier for me to decide whether to go back and live abroad."

On the eve of the meeting day, in assembly, Mr Stephens asked the pupils to remind their parents about the meeting. He also mentioned the Councillor's visit and reminded the students to be on their best behaviour that day.

I was one of the twelve ushers appointed by the new teacher to show the guests to the meeting hall. We all reported at the school premises at 3:30 pm in our spritely, pressed school uniforms, looking smarter than we'd ever looked. We could hear the buzz on the street as the people made their final preparations to welcome the Regional Councillor.

At 4:30 pm, the time of the meeting, only three people had been ushered into the hall where the teacher was waiting. Grandpa was one of them.

Mr Oriola had set up displays with maps and drawings to show the people some of his ideas. He paced up and down the back of the hall, a deep contemplative scowl on his face.

At about 5 pm, we heard cheering noises in the street. The Councillor had arrived. It was obvious our meeting was a resounding flop, and we were expecting the teacher to tell us to go home. I felt terribly sorry for him, and genuinely sad for my people.

Then something strange happened. The noise grew louder, and an unexpected mob arrived at the school gate. Within a short time, an endless flow of babbling villagers proceeded up to the school hall. The entire assembly hall was soon packed to the rafters. People stood outside, listening to the proceedings of the meeting broadcast through a reverberating megaphone. All the old men and women had something to say, and all were cheered loudly for their contributions. The whole event went on late into the night.

The fact was that the Councillor had failed to turn up that day, and had outraged the villagers by sending his junior assistant instead.

Not a wise move.

That event was a landmark in the history of our village. For me, however, it was the extraordinary man who put me on the path to a successful career as a doctor, unwittingly setting himself on a direct course to replace the Regional Councillor.

In Another World

There was a shape under the sheets, at the same spot where I'd just sprung up, right beside Helena. A pile of duvet, perhaps. Or pillows. I sometimes slept with pillows laced lengthwise to assuage those telltale niggling pains. Fringe detriments of being middle aged. My hands trembled as I lifted the bed sheet, and I almost fainted at what I saw. There was someone underneath, and *that person* was me. I was looking at my own face and hands, as though I was looking at someone else. *His* eyes were closed, and his hands were clasped across his chest. I could hear my heart pounding, and my throat hurt as I swallowed uncontrollably.

What's the meaning of this?

When I stroked his hands, they were cold and heavy. I held him by the shoulders and shook him, but he didn't open his eyes. I grabbed a handful of his shaggy brown hair and slapped him hard across the face. A large, mottled pink patch formed on his left cheek and spread slowly down towards his neck, but he remained motionless. My lungs started pumping in short, shallow puffs. I was running out of breath, or so I thought. My stomach was threatening to flip.

Calm down, Toby. You're a rational being. You must know that this is a dream.

A stupid, stupid dream.

I was no stranger to weird dreams. Once I had a dream in which I was the guest of honour at an underwater dinner party. I was wearing a double-breasted black suit and a fedora, and conversing attentively with a very attractive but incredibly talkative stainless steel teapot named Sarah. However, I was normally able to tell when I was in a dream, and if I didn't like the way it was playing out I'd shake myself awake. Even in my sleep I was conscious of what was real and what wasn't.

Helena was still sleeping. I was surprised she hadn't woken up during my assault on the body lying next to her, as she was usually a light sleeper. I peered at her face and was shocked by the pallid quality and curious peacefulness of her features.

Oh God! She's not breathing!

Panic welled in my gut, shot up my spine like an electric current, sending my head spinning.

What the heck's going on?

I shook her roughly by the shoulders and shouted. "Helena! Helena! Helena!"

Then something hit me and sent my panic into overdrive. Although I'd been yelling at the top of my voice, I couldn't hear myself - I was as silent as a goldfish. I exploded into silent laughter. This was clearly a dream, and I was about to wake up. I tried to shake myself awake, but to no avail.

In the bathroom, I resisted the urge to urinate. If this was a dream, the last thing I wanted was to wake up and find I'd done it on the bed! I splashed some water on my face, but the water felt like fine sand. It brushed my skin, ran through my fingers and bounced around in the washbasin. I stared into the sink, astonished.

When I looked in the mirror, I knew something was amiss, but I couldn't work out what it was. The rough blue towel draped on the door hook behind me didn't cover an area where the paint had been peeling off. Another chore to do at the weekend. Best to repaint the door before Helena started complaining about it. As it was, her complaints list was almost out of control. The kitchen door was not shutting properly, the ironing board was starting to wobble, the external TV aerial needed adjusting, the bath's hot water tap was leaking, and there was a faint smell of smoke in the kitchen, even when she wasn't cooking. Helena always noticed these things and whined constantly about the tiniest issues. In fact, I'd concluded long ago that she was happiest when she was complaining.

I suddenly realized what was amiss with the mirror. It did not reflect my image. There was nobody there!

That gave me such a fright. For a fraction of a second, I thought my heart would burst. Blood rushed to my head and nausea overwhelmed me. I thought I was going to faint. I clutched at my chest with one hand and steadied myself against the bathroom sink with the other. As my vision cleared, I looked again at the mirror, horrified. I could see the door and everything behind me, but there was no *me* in the mirror. I was invisible. The beginnings of a scream gathered force in my throat, but nothing came out. I yanked the towel off the door and wiped my face. A small relief; I might be invisible but at least I was solid - I could feel my face.

I ran to Richard and Michelle's bedroom. Both their beds were empty. I couldn't take it anymore. I leapt down the steps to the ground floor of our town house and stopped short. Helena was on the long sofa, curled up like a kitten, vigorously dabbing her wide, pale blue eyes with soggy tissue paper. Her Bible was by her side and she held a rosary in her hands. I rushed over and swept my arms around her.

My voice was shaking and my mouth was dry. "What's wrong, Helena? Where are the children?" It was strange just to hear my own voice again.

"I can't find the kitchen," she sobbed.

"What do you mean, you can't find the kitchen?"

A feeble flame danced in her eyes, and her glistening forehead reflected the strange light coming from outside. Her lips trembled and she clutched the rosary like a lifeline, rattling off Hail Marys in quick succession. The only time I'd seen her so ruffled was the day we took a ride on the Brighton pier roller coaster. "Never again," she'd declared immediately afterwards.

I barged into a chair on my way to where the kitchen should have been. She sniffed and glared at me. Even in her distress, she couldn't overlook my awkwardness. She'd often remarked that even when there was no obstacle, I'd imagine one just so I could trip over it. I was her clumsy "Professor Clumps".

I found myself pacing up and down next to the wall that divided the kitchen from the dining area. I tasted blood. I'd bitten into my lip. I felt like punching the wall.

"Where's the bloody kitchen, for Christ's sake?"

Helena brought her hands, rosary and all, to her face. "Please, don't..." she pleaded.

If there was one thing my wife couldn't stand, it was calling the Lord's name in vain. I'd only muttered it, but Helena's ears were phenomenally sensitive to blasphemous utterances. In fact, her religious sensibilities were so finely tuned she could hear a gnat fart from a hundred miles.

"I don't know what's happening, dear, but I can't find the kitchen either," I finally had to admit.

"You don't know what's happening?" She sniffed and dabbed her eyes. "Can't you see?"

"Ah, of course, let me guess," I jibed. "It's the end of the world, right?"

The alabaster sheen on her face paled even more, and her countenance assumed a dreamlike quality. I could see she was about to go 'Pentecostal' on me, which I dreaded more than her inventory of complaints.

"And they shall be taken up..." she sighed.

"Look, Helena, let's not go into any of your Pentecostal mumbo-jumbo today. All this... It's just a silly dream."

"So, whose dream is it then; yours or mine?" she snapped.

"Okay, you'll see..." I bit hard on my arm until it hurt like hell, but that didn't wake me. I gripped my nose firmly between my thumb and my index finger, and I held my breath until I was about to pass out.

Helena finally began to show some interest in my antics.

"You should try walking into the wall. If you can walk right through it, then it's a dream. Or why don't you just jump up and see if you can fly!"

"Why don't *you* try?" I replied.

"Don't be ridiculous," she countered indignantly.

"Okay, so it's not a dream, what is it then?"

"It's the end of the world, dear, and the Lord is taking his own to be with him. We who are still alive will be caught up together in the clouds..."

"So you reckon the children have been caught up?" I asked, looking out of the window in mock despair.

"... I tell you, on that night two people will be in one bed; one will be taken and the other left."

"Yeah, so why have you not been taken? As you happen to be Mother Teresa, and the rest of us are all but bloody infidels. And how does that explain the missing kitchen? Has that been taken up as well? I guess they'll need the kitchen up there more than we do."

"The Bible says in the last days there will be an increase in the number of people like you who don't believe in the signs - 2 Peter 3, Verse 4."

She was now riffling through her Bible with trembling hands.

"You can't fool me with any of that nonsense. I attended a Catholic school, remember?"

"… The sun will become dark, and the moon will turn to blood."

"Hmm, I wonder what Jeremiah was smoking when he came up with that one."

"That wasn't Jeremiah, it was Joel. And this is no time for blasphemy."

"Sure, but what happened to Armageddon? Did we miss that one? What's coming next?"

"The righteous shall…"

"Listen, Helena. I have an alternative hypothesis. One that is far more credible than yours…"

She shook her head and turned away.

"… I think, somehow, we have become trapped in a hidden dimension, in hyperspace."

"Of course, the nonsense of universal theoretical physics, in which everything is made out of invisible strings." She made a sound that was halfway between a giggle and a sob.

"Snigger away all you want, Helena. You wait until I have fully developed my theory. Look at the hands of the clock. They've been moving backwards since we got here. We've entered the realm of relativity and we're stuck behind a virtual wall in a Riemannian manifold."

"How can you believe such crap?" Helena wailed.

"Don't let's even begin to talk about the pile of contradictions in your own theory."

However, I wasn't particularly confident about my own theory, either. What sort of scientific deductions can you make when you stand directly in front of a mirror and can't see yourself? So far, the only thing that had kept me grounded was the weird sense that all this had happened before.

"You do know, of course, that there is valid mathematical proof for the behaviour of time, energy and matter in hyperspace."

"OK, tell me, Nutty Professor, at what point did we enter into this wonderful hyperspace dimension of yours?"

"Hmm... A very good question... But no matter how hard I try, I can't remember beyond... The more I try to work it out, the harder I find it to determine that point of reference. Where were we yesterday?"

"Ah, perhaps there is no yesterday in hyperspace. Bet you haven't thought of that, have you?"

She was laughing at me, but I didn't mind.

"We should expect to see some evidence of the string theory. As an object traverses the space-time field... Wait, if hyperspace is a discontinuous domain, the kitchen may well be situated on the other side of the universe..."

"...Or in a different time frame altogether," she jibed. "And our dear children may be stuck in the Jurassic Age, staring hopelessly into the eyes of a vicious and hungry T. Rex!"

"Helena, this is serious stuff, you know. The normal laws of physics don't apply in hyperspace. Time may become elastic - stretch and bend back upon itself..."

"Oh, please stop it, Toby... The trouble with you scientists is when your tests don't add up, you change the meaning of everyday concepts of time and space to suit your ridiculous theories. Really, sometimes you people sound like the folk of the olden days who thought a person could fall over the edge of the Earth..."

I couldn't hear the rest because suddenly there was an ear-piercing vibration, very much like the noise from the Large Hadron Collider in the middle of its energizing phase, but much louder. Our house was hurtling through a turbulent magnetic field. It became even brighter outside, so much so that the curtains emitted visible energy waves. Then there was a loud screech and an almighty flash that blinded me temporarily.

When my eyes recovered their function, Helena was gone.

"Helena!" I screamed hopelessly. The shrill sound that came out of my throat was a caricature of my own voice.

"Where the hell are you?"

This time there was no protest against my indulgent profanity. It seemed my wife had evaporated, leaving behind just a pile of dull ash.

The whole house suddenly became quiet.

Gone were the usual sounds of crockery and cutlery clinking in the kitchen; the jarring din of Michelle, wailing her lungs out in her playpen while Richard tried to placate her; the background noise of the TV and the pounding of feet up and down the wooden stairs.

My throat ached with a dull pain.

Has she really been taken up, and the children too?

Golden light streamed through the window, casting ominous patterns that danced on the wall. The TV and the hi-fi unit wore a shimmering halo of pink and blue. I was sure it would all eventually make sense, but the rumble that immediately followed filled me with apprehension and dread. My scalp prickled and my eyes stung with sweat. I had no doubt my blood pressure would be stuck firmly to the ceiling.

Christ! How much more of this can I take?

Then I suddenly realized I was in pain. The pain had been there all along, but I hadn't noticed. It bored into my chest and spread like fire up to my throat. Maybe Helena was right after all. I was on my way to hell. But I still couldn't see any sense in the whole idea of life after death. Everybody knows that the sensation of awareness is generated in the brain. So, once that is kaput and your vital organs have shut down - once your nerves are no longer carrying any signals - how can you possibly register any form of consciousness? It would be like expecting a piece of software to carry on functioning long after the computer has been switched off. That's just insane.

But the pain only worsened. My innards felt as if they were being fed through a high-quality commercial paper shredder. Perhaps I could still save myself.

But from what?

Helena's voice called faintly from a distance, her relentless refrain ringing in my ear: "For God so loved the world he gave his only begotten son, so that whoever believes in him shall not perish…"

How ridiculous is that?

To me spirituality was purely the domain of primeval imagination and fantasy. It would require a quantum leap and a large dose of self-delusion for me to believe that God was anything other than Santa for grown-ups.

Those contrarian thoughts were soon driven aground by an even more excruciating pain. It felt as if someone had ripped my eyes out of their sockets and then set fire to my lungs. If this is a taste of hell, oh, please give me Pascal's Wager. Self-delusion and mediocrity are a small price to pay for sure relief from perpetual torment. When the pain threshold is crossed, reality gives way to grey areas where logic and reasoning become irrelevant. The laws of relativity give way to the dictates of chaos.

Interspersed with my pain and my terror of looming annihilation was my fear and anxiety for my family. What has happened to Helena and the children? What is going to happen to me next? I was at the very limit of my endurance. This was the end. Something snapped inside my head. The surrounding light dimmed slowly. It felt like my consciousness was being sucked into a black hole.

At first, I thought I was lying in a field. I felt a cool breeze on my face. I heard voices, but I could neither move nor open my eyes. The noisome aroma of a hospital ward nudged me back to full reality.

"I think he's coming round," a man's voice said. I felt a hand on my forehead. "Dr McDonald, don't worry, you just relax. Everything is fine."

I could feel a dull pain in my chest and my throat. But a sudden jolt kicked off a strident hammering in my brain, and I found myself gripping the side of the narrow bed I was on.

What the hell happened? Where are the children? Where is Helena?

Then I heard a voice I thought I recognized. It seemed to come from beyond the boundaries of sense and perception.

"Phew! What a relief! Can we see him now?"

"Helena!"

I forced my eyes open. The effort caused a minor tsunami in my head, and I felt faint again.

"Daddy!"

Michelle's voice was the sound of music.

Helena threw her arms round my neck. "We've been praying for you all day!" Her pale blue eyes glistened like a sample of copper sulphate in a Petri dish. "Dear, you had carbon monoxide poisoning while you were sleeping. A gas leak from underneath the hubs in the kitchen... Good thing the children and I had gone to Mum and Dad's for the weekend!"

I sighed, and then I whispered, "Thank God!"

My Name is Jerry

At first I didn't notice the man standing at the door. Even when he began to speak, I still frantically hunted for the ventriloquist prankster around me. I finally looked down only when I heard David from behind me say, "Hi!" All I could see was an unwieldy mop of greying hair on an adult head, assuming a polite salute at the height of the brass buckle of my favourite Journeyman plaited leather belt. I stood back, pushing little David further inside. Only then did I get a full view of the small owner of the surprisingly deep, theatrical voice. A pair of vacant lacklustre brown eyes stared pleadingly from his hungry face, on which rested an overgrown bushy moustache and a forlorn pair of wiry eyebrows that dated him in his 50s. He had on a greasy, dark brown, oversized duffel coat with missing buttons over a stained shirt and a pair of turned-up black trousers. I could not concentrate on his appeals properly because David was pushing past my legs, struggling to get between the stranger and me.

"Kindly give me some drinking water, please?" the man repeated, performing a gesture of drinking from an invisible cup.

The request didn't immediately register with me. Even afterwards, I still marvelled at how unusual it was for someone to turn up at my doorstep asking for a drink of water in the middle of Bexley. It had never happened before, and I had no contingency plan for handling such an unlikely event. Salesmen, Jehovah's Witnesses, or even burglars I could deal with quite proficiently, but this situation presented an entirely new dilemma. Why didn't he go to the newsagent down the road and get himself a bottle of Perrier?

"Hey, come right in." David had taken over. "What's your name?"

"I'm Jerry. You're quite fat for a child." The man wriggled his moustache at David, who laughed.

Jerry sat on the settee close to the door.

I fixed David with a reproachful stare. Jane and I had warned him over and over again to keep away whenever there was a stranger at the door. There was so much crime about, and at that time there was an ongoing scare of a very young criminal terrorizing the neighbourhood and giving the police the runaround.

I dashed into the kitchen to get the stranger a glass of water.

"Who's that?" Jane called from the bathroom upstairs.

I was still working out what to say when David shouted, "It's a little man, Mum! Can we keep him?"

"David!" I yelled after him as he sprinted up the stairs. Then I glanced at our unexpected guest, who smiled to reassure me that he was not offended by the boy's comment. For his lack of height and condition of penury, he seemed remarkably at ease. Under the same circumstances, I felt certain I'd be a bitter, twisted soul.

I wanted him to drink up quickly and go, since I didn't want to have to explain to Jane that I'd let someone into the house without her ascertaining that everything was in order. In most cases, the place was okay anyway, but she still had to make a little fuss, dusting the pictures or fluffing the pillows on the settees before anyone could come into the house.

The sound of footsteps grew louder on the stairs - Jane's light, graceful bound and David's rapid pit-pat. The little man had drunk only half of the water. He stretched out his miniature limbs in an exaggerated gesture of relaxation and relief.

"Oh, thanks for that," he said. "My throat was absolutely on fire."

I just stood there and watched helplessly while he embarked on another prolonged swig. Eyes tightly closed, brows slanted downward like the arms of cartoon arrowheads, and his moustache - the playful squirrel attached to his upper lip - wriggled in time to the oscillations of his wizened Adam's apple. I resigned myself to my impending fate and braced myself for the outburst that was sure to come when Jane set her eyes on the tramp in her sitting room.

"Chris! What is this man doing in our house?" Her contempt was undisguised, and her voice was hiked well above its normal volume.

"He's only stopped in for a drink of water."

"Why doesn't he get his water somewhere else? Our house is not some sort of watering hole for stray vagrants." She stomped off to the kitchen.

I knew what was coming next, and I braced myself once again.

"...And who left bread crumbs all over the worktop and filthy dishes in the sink?"

Jane's kitchen was a temple, and leaving plates in the sink was akin to defecating on the sacred altar of the most high.

"It's me," I apologized, joining her in the kitchen to assure her that I planned to restore the place to its normal pristine condition."

"You've got to make him go!" Her whisper was a grating, harsh rasp. "I know his sort. He's going to want to stay."

"Of course he's not staying. He only wanted a drink of water."

"You silly fool, you shouldn't have let him in. You should have made him stay outside and taken the water to him there."

I shrugged. I should have thought of that at the time but I wasn't as clever as Jane. I normally didn't react in such a timely fashion, which was why she was a head teacher at the local primary school and I worked as a lowly porter in the post office depot.

"Don't worry. He'll go once he's finished drinking."

David arrived at the scene. He tried to fill the kitchen doorway, and stared at us with pursed lips. His legs were planted slightly apart, and his little clenched fists were pressed against his hips as if he was ready for a fight. I glowered back at him, and he quickly stepped aside to let me pass by into the living room.

Jerry was still sitting there. His wonky smile had an immediate disarming effect. "You wouldn't happen to have some biscuits or other munchies I could throw at the raging hyenas in my poor little stomach?" He had a pleading look in his eye that couldn't possibly be ignored.

"Okay," I said, feeling rather deflated. "I'll get you some biscuits, and then you must be on your way." I waited, but he just stared at me with those dull, pitiful eyes.

Jane watched as I opened the biscuit tin and shoved a handful into a small polythene carrier bag. She didn't speak, but the angry glint in her eyes said volumes.

The man reached for the bag with a shaking hand, but he remained seated despite my attempt to entice him to stand up and come for it. I reckoned that if I could get him on to his feet, he'd soon be on his way. But he just sat there with his hand stretched out, rather like a command from an elderly person to a younger man. In the end, the seniority sentiment won; I'd been brought up always to obey my elders.

He opened the bag with trembling hands and stuffed his mouth in a frenzy, causing the crumbs to scatter all over Jane's precious Turkmen Saryk rug. I winced and glanced nervously towards the kitchen door.

"Ooooh..." Jerry beamed, "The rodents in my tummy send their sincere thanks. Here, come and listen..."

This was immediately followed by a fit of uncontrolled laughter from the dining area.

"David!"

David calmed down and then looked at me with large pleading eyes. "Please Dad, can't we keep him?"

"Shush! Don't talk about him like that. He's not a dog."

Once again, I shot an apologetic glance at the man.

"Anyway, he can't stay here. We have no spare room for a guest."

The little man sobered up and donned a plaintive mask of dejection.

"But Dad," begged David, "he can stay in my room."

"Please, let me stay," pleaded the vagrant. "Just for tonight, and then I'll be on my way. It's pretty cold out there, especially at night. I could sleep in your bath. I'll be mighty comfy in there."

I thought for a moment about the unkempt midget lying snugly in the bath. Jane's £2000 Excelsior bath! That would be like pissing on the Golden Fleece. I coughed to stave off the laughter that was rising in my throat. *If you do such a thing*, I thought, *you won't be mighty comfy, dear. You'll be mighty dead!*

I sighed. Of course, if it really came to it, he could always sleep in Henrietta's room. She was in college, and she only came home on alternate weekends. Jane had had Henrietta long before we met - the product of a heady, unbashful and irresponsible past. Henrietta was every bit as fiery as her mum. She didn't just have a bee in her bonnet; she had a humongous Megachile pluto, and a chip on both shoulders. David and I normally kept out of her way, especially when she and Jane were having their stormy moments. However, she'd been surprisingly agreeable in the previous couple of months. She seemed to have made a complete turnaround in her college work, and - amazingly - was looking forward to her final year results.

It wasn't easy persuading Jane to allow Jerry to stay for the night. She was waiting in the kitchen, her eyes blazing with contempt and rage. She had her back to the sink, and both her hands gripped the counter's edge while she glared coldly at me.

"You must get rid of him at once!" she snarled.

I was beginning to tire of her uncompromising lack of charity.

"I'm sorry, dear. I don't see how we can just chuck him out like that. Why not let him stay just for tonight? Tomorrow I'll arrange for him to go to a hostel or something."

"No, we can't have him here. We can't just have every troll strolling off the street into our house and staying the night. If you don't get rid of him at once, I'll call the police."

"Calm down now, Jane. The guy hasn't committed any crime."

Her delicate nostrils flared, and her chest heaved. I stepped forward and put my hands around her shoulders. She tried to push me away, but I refused to budge.

"Just what will David think of us if we kick the guy out? Can't you see that David has taken to the old tramp?"

Jane relaxed.

"Okay, so where's he going to sleep? There's no way I'll have him sleeping in Henrietta's room."

"Why not? It's only going to be for tonight, after all. We don't have to tell Henrietta about it, do we?"

She sighed and broke loose from my hold.

"I don't like this one bit. We don't even know him. What if he's a psycho? What if he gets up in the night, strangles one of us and makes off with your CD collection? Or what if he dies in his sleep? What would you do then?"

"Don't worry, Jane. Trust me. It's going to be OK."

In the next couple of hours, we queried Jerry about his life and background, hoping to extract some useful information to help us decide where to take him the next day. We had little success; the only thing we found out was that his name was Jerry Cann. Beyond that, all we got was a long rambling fable that led us in and out of an intricate maze of what could only have been the work of pure imagination from a precariously unstable mind. David, though, was immensely entertained.

Jerry excused himself to the bathroom. He was in there for over an hour, performing a raucous rendition of the *Umpa Lumpa* song to the accompaniment of the sound of splashing water.

By this time, Jane's fury had mellowed. She tidied up Henrietta's room, put a new sheet on the bed, and turned up the radiator a notch. But she remained unfriendly and suspicious towards the little man, and she kept a guarded distance from him.

"I told you, Chris. He's been making it difficult for us to know anything about him. I'm sure that's not his real name. He's taking you for a fool."

Once again, I assured her that it'll be okay. One night was all he was going to spend here. That was it.

I was wrong. The next day was a Monday. Jerry was still in bed by the time I left for work, and I didn't want to wake him, so I left some toast and egg on the dining table for his breakfast. Jane and David had left before me. Jane had left with the ultimatum that Jerry must be out of the house before she returned at 4 pm.

On Tuesday, I promised that I'd definitely book him into the YMCA on Albert Street, but it turned out they didn't have any spare beds. By Wednesday, Jane was pretty much resigned to the idea of having Jerry around. He'd become best pals with David, who couldn't miss Jerry's bedtime reading, which was pure entertainment as Jerry wove his own ideas into the stories in the books and made the characters truly come alive. Moreover, in the space of just three days, David's interest in numeracy had gone right through the ceiling. With Jerry's help, he was doing long multiplications and recursive divisions. David had become so fond of Jerry. He was always offering the little old man half of the food on his plate because he thought his small stature was the result of not eating enough. But Jane was always there to warn David. "If you don't eat your vegetables, you now know what could happen to you," she'd say, casting a sidelong glance in Jerry's direction. Then David would quickly shovel his veggies into his mouth, chomp without passion, and force himself to swallow.

We still didn't know much about Jerry, and it was up to me to find out more. Finally, on the fifth day, while David and Jane were safely out of the way, I resolved to get some answers. Slumped on the settee, looking very much at home, Jerry watched Jeremy Kyle on ITV. He was so relaxed one would have thought he was part of the family.

"Jerry."

The seriousness of my tone immediately hit him. His face suddenly tensed up, and a sudden panic flashed in his beady eyes, but it was only for a brief moment.

"We don't know enough about you, Jerry. We need to know who you are so we can get you settled. You can't live with us forever, you know."

"Let me tell you about the time in Timbuktu when I made balloon shapes out of a rattlesnake..."

"No, Jerry," I quickly cut in, determined not to be drawn into another one of his intriguing tales. I said firmly, "What I want to know is who you really are. Where did you come from? How old are you? Where is your family? How did you find yourself on Grosvenor Park Road?"

"Erm... If I told you that, then I'll have to kill you," he chuckled nervously.

"No, Jerry. Don't give me any of that crap. I'm dead serious, I need some answers from you this time. If you don't spit it out, I'll have to leave it to Jane to conduct this interrogation."

The saddest possible look came upon his wrinkled face. His squirrel moustache drooped limply, and his eyes welled up with tears. He swallowed hard, and I could see the struggle in his eyes as he considered his next words.

"I'm afraid, Chris, the truth is I have no answer to any of your questions. I try terribly hard, but I can't remember anything."

I glared at him incredulously. At first, I thought he was still trying to be evasive, but when I stopped to consider his plight, I realized that it made sense. This would explain the glazed, vacant look that often occupied his face. I'd often wondered why he kept stumbling while recalling names, sometimes even David's name. When Jane asked him what his shoe size was, we were amazed at the confusion that overwhelmed him, the way he scratched his head in puzzlement before he finally admitted that he didn't know his own shoe size.

"It's so difficult," he lamented with pained eyes. "I can't remember anything. The harder I try, the more confused I get. I've since given up trying to remember what happened yesterday. Now, I just take each day as it comes."

I concluded that there was no point harassing the poor bloke any more than was necessary. But it raised some questions, and it was clear that we'd have to get some help with his selective amnesia, which somehow hadn't rendered him completely useless. Otherwise, how did he manage to read to David and help him out with his maths work? I'd personally been a fortunate beneficiary of some sound advice from the old chap when I confided in him about the concerns I was having at the depot. I'd been singled out for a transfer and certain demotion, and he told me to ask my superintendent about my competency and attendance record. I did, and that led to the revelation that I was the only one who had never called in sick or missed training. I wasn't a lazy worker, and it could be proved that the management was being unfair.

Amnesia or not, Jerry was an intelligent old man.

And now, he was almost part of the family. I'd even heard Jane laugh at his crooked jokes once or twice.

"Nonsense!" snorted Jane when I told her later that day about what I had learned. "If you're not going to throw him out, then I'll make the call to the police myself. Goodness knows what he's hiding from, and when it all comes out, you may find that we've been harbouring a hardened criminal. If he's not out of this house by the time we get back from school tomorrow, I'm going straight to the police."

But he still wasn't gone the following day when they got back home. Seeing him, David ran gleefully into Jerry's arms and gave him a hug. Jane's resolve withered, and she abandoned her threat. Later that evening, after David and Jerry had turned in for the night, Jane and I discussed the matter over a late supper.

"He does seem to be genuinely amnesic," Jane conceded. "That dead look in his eyes; it can't possibly be faked. But what can we do?"

Since he'd first arrived, we'd already conducted some discreet enquiries around the neighbourhood. The Indian shopkeeper at the local grocery stores had seen him around for some time but had no idea where he'd come from. The newsagent on Belvedere Road said that Jerry had once popped in, but he'd had to shoo him on when he was apparently getting in the way of his customers. Beyond that, no-one knew anything about him. So in the end we decided to put an ad in *The Bexley Advertiser*; someone in the catchment area of the local paper was bound to know of him.

We didn't get any response to our local ad until two days after placing it. At first, I was quite excited when a frenzied female voice crackled over the phone in what sounded like a long-distance call. "We're extremely relieved you've got him and that he's safe and well. I've been sick with worry... and so have his six brothers too!"

When she said her name was Snow White, I was

thoroughly disappointed, and I promptly slammed the phone down.

The only person who saw the humour in the story was Jerry. "Ah! Snow White, of course. You don't want to know the sort of things we got up to; us naughty little midgets and the lovely Snow White," he guffawed.

"Knock it off, Jerry," I scolded, aware of the perplexed frown on David's little face.

None of us had remembered to tell Henrietta about our strange guest who had taken up residence in her bedroom. One day, Henrietta breezed in without warning while Jane was away at a late PTA meeting. David and I were downstairs watching Wallace and Gromit. No-one heard her come in and go upstairs to her room to unpack. We only realized she was in the house when we heard her piercing scream as she flew down the stairs.

"Heeeeeeeeeeeeeeeeek! What's he doing in my bed?"

I'd never seen her look so pale. Her eyes bulged to twice their normal size, and she shivered in spite of her purple fur coat.

I went round and put my hand on her shoulder to soothe her. "Sorry, Etta, he's our guest. We thought he'd be gone by now. We should have called you..."

But that didn't calm her down. If only Jane had been there; she alone could have handled the situation. David and I looked on helplessly as Henrietta broke down in an uncontrollable fit of hysteria, her screams piercing through the whole place like a burglar alarm.

But the ever-increasing look of panic that overcame

her face as Jerry descended the stairs told me that there was more to Henrietta's distress than the shock of finding a stranger in her bedroom.

"What - what is he doing here?" she whimpered when Jerry came into full view.

David and I were shocked to see that he wasn't quite the same Jerry that we knew. He'd shaved his beard and moustache, and he was wearing a pair of jeans and a white T-shirt. When he spoke, we were doubly shocked to find that even his voice was different from his usual hoarse baritone. This was a far younger Jerry, only in his late 20s.

"Sorry, Etta," he said. "I didn't mean to freak you out." The only thing that hadn't changed was the fleeting vacant lustre in his eye - and of course that he was still a dwarf.

He continued, "I had no choice. I couldn't understand why you wouldn't return my calls."

"Get away from me!" Henrietta screeched.

"What the hell is going on here?" I heard myself shouting.

"I helped her with her college project, and she promised that if she passed with top marks..." he looked in David's direction and held his tongue.

"What was the promise?" I inquired.

The little man shrugged and pulled a face. Then he drew near and whispered into my ear. A fleeting image of obscenity flashed through my mind.

"What... Don't be silly!"

Then he turned pleadingly to Henrietta. "Please,

Etta, just once, that's all I ask!"

I sought Henrietta's averted eyes. "This is utterly ridiculous. Is he telling the truth? You really promised...?"

She only whimpered and clenched her fists as if she was in anguish.

"Look," I said, "this has nothing to do with me. I'm leaving this for your mum to deal with when she gets back home."

I turned to David, who was sitting at the dining table, watching the unfolding scene with the dazed expression of a kid who had stumbled upon a stash of lewd magazines in his grandfather's bedroom.

"Come on, kiddo. It's bedtime. I'll come upstairs in a moment and read you a story."

And, for the first time, David went to his bedroom without any fuss.

"I want you to get out of here before my mum comes in," Henrietta spat at Jerry.

But he'd already sat down, and it was clear that he wouldn't budge.

"If you don't leave, I will call the police."

I switched off the TV and sat down. Jerry turned and stared at the floor when I looked at him. I was still trying to deal with the mixed feelings I had about him. I wasn't sure whether he deserved an Oscar for his excellent impersonation or a slap across the face for his deceit.

We were each jolted out of our thoughts when a knock came at the door. Although Jane carried her keys, she often preferred to be let in. As I went to open the door, I could feel Henrietta's anxiety. It crackled in the air like an electric spark.

"He's here, isn't he?"

It was the stern voice of a police officer. I immediately noticed the blue flashing lights on a couple of vans on the road a few doors away from our house. At the same time, I heard the sound of a scuffle inside, and I realized that Jerry was trying to make a dash for the back door. Alas, his little legs could only carry him so far. The officer was upon him in a flash, shackling him immediately with a pair of fine brass cuffs.

The policeman addressed him. "You managed to slip from our grasp two weeks ago, but this time you're coming with me to the nick. You were seen breaking into a maisonette, three doors away, and there have been reports of your activities in this area."

Jerry wriggled helplessly as he was dragged away, but not before casting a final baleful glance in Henrietta's direction.

Henrietta disappeared up the stairs, leaving me in the lounge to wonder whether to feel sorry for Jerry or wish that he would rot in custody. I did not get enough time to settle the score in my mind, since Jane arrived, just in time to see the police lead Jerry out of the door.

Hand of Fate

Congratulating myself that I'd successfully located the Indian Restaurant called *The Marok*, I took a table that gave me an oblique view of the busy Harlem Street, and then I waited. The place must have been too comfy because I nodded off almost immediately.

When I next opened my eyes it was 3:30 pm.

My mouth was filled with the metallic taste that I'd come to associate with instant panic. My immediate thought was that he'd been there, failed to see me, and stormed off in a rage. Even after the waiter assured me that nobody had turned up in the past hour, I didn't feel relief. Instead, all I felt was that familiar, awful ache in my chest. I'd got it all wrong yet again! My random blackouts and unaccountable bouts of amnesia were a curse that would blight my life forever.

"May I use your phone to make a quick call?"

Without once taking his eyes off mine, the waiter solemnly advised that there was a pay phone just down the road. His tired, middle-aged face remained politely blank. So off I went, struggling into my brown mohair jacket as I blundered out of the door.

The person I was meeting was supposed to be the source of a severely craved all-in-one breakfast and lunch. My tank had long fallen below reserve, and I was already digesting my own guts. A lousy 50p was all I had to my name; just enough to make a phone call. I drummed on the battered dusty coin box in the phone booth with my chapped fingers as the phone purred at the other end. I prayed desperately. If I got his voice mail there'd be no point in leaving a message because I didn't have a contact number. After several rings, I resigned myself to my well-accustomed bad luck and was about to hang up when the line suddenly came alive. It crackled briefly, and then the savage blast of his irate voice took my unwary ear by surprise.

"Where the hell are you? I've been waiting here for the past thirty minutes!"

Even after I blurted out my excuses - surely I was where I thought we'd arranged - he still screamed down the phone at me.

"*The Hallam Cuisine* on Terry Street. That's what I said, you grinning idiot! If you don't get your dumb arse right here in the next twenty minutes I'll be gone, and that'll be the end of it."

For once, I finally sussed out that this bastard was messing me about. I was sure he hadn't said *The Hallam Cuisine*. If he had, I'd have known it. There was no way I'd confused *The Hallam* with another restaurant. I knew the place; I'd been there twice before, and I never wanted to go there again.

It was a Friday, about two weeks before. I picked up a card at the job centre in Lewisham. The sleepy-eyed HR administrator arranged an interview for me with the manager of *The Hallam Cuisine*. Temp kitchen porter. That was the extent of my aspirations. I didn't have the bus fare that day, but I found my way there all the same. Weary, I stood in front of the wood-framed glass door and watched the only two punters inside the restaurant. One of them was wearing a black French suit and a red tie, his jet black hair carefully raked back and parted in front, his gold watch glinting as he moved his hand about. The other guy was in a black T-shirt and a pair of blue jeans. Unlike the first bloke, he was slightly overweight and entirely bald. It was like watching a scene from *The Godfather* or *The Sopranos*, and I soon found myself fully immersed in the unfolding plot.

Ben's face radiates with the full flush of his irresistible charm. His manicured hands perform an impressive flurry of gesticulations as he enthrals his listener across the other side of the table. His poise and bravado have been perfectly honed over his many years as a top-class fixer, blagger extraordinaire, and consummate wheeler-dealer in the backstreets of Birmingham, from where he'd eventually found it necessary to make a hasty getaway.

Richard's attentiveness is merely an act that he doesn't intend to carry on for long. His mission is to size up Ben before seeing him off from the neighbourhood. This smug young fool has sunk his talons into the only daughter of back-street billionaire Simon Bellows, and he's making her life a misery as a result of his wayward ways.

"Wave a wad under his greedy nose and make him go away" was the instruction of the esteemed veteran gangster, anxious to protect his beloved daughter without her suspecting his hand in the matter. Although Richard knows other, more effective, ways of making people disappear, he's bound by a debt of gratitude to the only man in the world he fears and respects.

Richard has never met this scoundrel until now, but he has no concern about the outcome of this assignation: The numskull will accept the offer and clear off the scene like the greedy swine he is.

But, as soon as Richard sets his eyes on Ben, the entire showcase turns upside down. Now look who's turned up! *Immediately absorbing the initial shock and maintaining a blank face.* It's James, the swindler of Birmingham. *This slimy little crook owed him more than 20 grand, yet he managed to escape with his limbs intact. And now, by some quirky dint of good fortune, he's been delivered into Richard's hands. But, for now, he can't afford to get excited. They must both keep up this ridiculous charade while within earshot of other people.*

Ben has now realized what he's walked into, but he maintains a straight face. He knows he's staring into the eyes of Big Ricky, the guy who sent the hounds after him three years ago; the reason he'd fled Birmingham in the first place and since lived under a variety of false identities.

He continues to smile at the fat sucker in front of him

and prattle on about the merits of the Z-tech security system, which is what he thought he'd be clinching another fraudulent commission for. Nothing on his charming face betrays the wild churning that's going on inside his stomach or the erratic pulsations hammering away in his cowardly chest.

"Yes, of course...Indeed...Who'd have thought?" Richard reels out his automatic interjections, but behind his flat snake-like eyes, he is calmly plotting a fitting torture for this smooth-talking little thief. Back in Birmingham, he was always playing the big shot; living in expensive hotels, drinking champagne, and chasing after posh broads.

But, of course, this isn't about the 20 grand; that's peanuts. It's about honour and respect, and James - or Ben, or whatever else he calls himself - has crossed the line, and now he's going to get what's coming to him.

I was jolted out of my trance by the appearance of the waitress. She swayed on her slender frame as she approached the men with a tray of red wine balanced on her palm. She opened the dark green bottle and decanted a small amount of wine in the glass of the younger man, who contorted his face curiously as he tasted, then smiled and nodded at the waitress, who proceeded to fill his glass.

Then disaster struck.

For some reason, she lurched forward and spilled the wine on the young man's suit. He leapt up as if he'd been scalded, and then performed frantic hand gestures and drew his face into the most horrific sneer. At first, the waitress remained transfixed, her lips forming a terrified O-shape. Then she suddenly recovered. She bowed her head as she backed away until she disappeared from view.

Her name was Niyati. She was from Nepal, but she preferred to tell people she came from India. I'd seen her first at the job centre and afterwards at the Lewisham library. Recently, it seemed she popped up everywhere, aloof and arrogant, staring at you with that withering sneer.

But James is up to his old tricks. As the waitress begins to pour the wine, he reaches from under the table and tugs at her skirt. She is startled. Her hand jerks forward, and she spills some wine on him.

"Bitch, you just ruined my suit!"

The waitress gasps, steps back and apologizes profusely. James' eyes glint as he turns to Richard. "A moment, please. I'll go to the gents to see what I can do to tidy up this mess." He stands up to leave, but the smirk on his face quickly disappears when Big Ricky gets up as well.

"Actually, I too need to use the john, so I'll come along with you."

How long I'd been standing at the restaurant door, I'll never know. I was startled when the waitress suddenly turned up at the door, staring at me with strange blazing eyes, her pretty face crumpled up into a mask of pure contempt.

"What the heck are you doing here?"

Although she had mouthed the words, I imagined

her voice - a piercing screech hitting the back of my skull like a burning spear. I muttered futilely that I had come to see the manager about a job, but she couldn't have heard from behind the glass door. She opened the door, and I could feel her breath searing my face.

"Get lost!" she hissed like a rattlesnake. Eyes still blazing, she retched up a large gob of phlegm which she spat directly in my face. It felt heavy and warm as it slid gently down my forehead, between my eyebrows, and down the spine of my nose. Then she turned round and walked away while I just stood there.

The manager came to the door. He was a squat Asian man with sad brown eyes, and was in his mid-thirties. I hadn't wiped my face, and the phlegm was now hanging pendulously from the tip of my nose.

"I - I've come about the vacancy," I stuttered.

"Sorry, mate. It's been filled." With that, he shut the door and drew the curtains.

Since then my mind had been invaded by strange visions in which the girl's pretty face had dissolved into a vivid mask of horror, and her sweet voice rang in a panicked scream, and there was blood everywhere.

Terry Street wasn't far; five minutes by bus, or fifteen minutes of brisk trudge. As I didn't have the bus fare, the latter was my only choice. Although I now knew it was all a scam, I was still determined to give this meeting one last go. I'd never met the guy; I didn't even know his name. But, if he's actually waiting for me at the restaurant, he could have some life-changing news, or at least there might be a meal in it for me.

It all started with an ad in the Lewisham local advertiser:

IF THIS IS YOU, THEN CALL 077554489

The gist of it: A young man had helped an old man off the bus and taken him over safely to the other side of the road. The kind-hearted fellow was now being sought, presumably for some sort of commendation.

I was sure it was me, but I didn't immediately call the number. I mulled it over for two weeks before finally plucking up the courage. When I called, I was taken aback at the strong Brummie accent of a young man at the other end of the line; a strangely familiar voice. Businesslike but polite, he asked a few questions about the incident: What was the old man wearing? What did he say? Where did he join the bus? Who else was there?

Unprepared for all the questioning, I suddenly froze. The phone turned into a rattlesnake, and I was about to drop it. But he sensed my panic and quickly explained that it wasn't a police investigation or anything like that. He just needed to confirm that he was talking to the right person. So I recounted everything I knew about the event. How I'd been on bus 433 heading towards Hackney, and the old man was sitting just opposite, gazing out of the window, how we'd both stopped at the Maryland Road bus stop, and how I'd helped him across the busy street.

The young man thanked me and said we should meet, but he didn't provide any additional information; it was up to me to fill in the gaps with my own imagination.

Perhaps the old man had croaked, and left some money in his will for the unknown young man who had restored his faith in humanity. Maybe my luck was about to shift; I could start a better life, get a decent job, attend evening school, get some qualifications, and join the police. I imagined myself turning up at home in Birmingham wearing a police uniform. It would give my old man a heart attack; the arrogant old crow who had declared that I'd end up in jail.

After walking for more than five minutes, I suddenly discovered that the jacket I was wearing wasn't mine. It was slightly bigger, and it had a smell. I put my hand in the pocket, and I quickly withdrew it because it felt strange and slippery in there. It was as if I'd put my hand in a wet, slimy crab hole. I thought about taking the jacket back to *The Marok*. Obviously, some forgetful turkey took my jacket and left his own in its place. But if I returned this jacket, I would probably never get mine back. Anyway, I didn't have anything valuable in my pockets, and this one was of better quality.

Past *The Baker's Arms* on Munro Street, I turned into Green Lane. Only five minutes until my appointment. I quickened my pace and assured myself that I'd get there in time. I put my hand in the pocket again, and this time I touched something. It was cold and wet with a slightly rough texture. I had a growing sense of unease as I felt it with my hand. Now severely apprehensive, but tremendously curious, I clasped it and thought it felt like - I couldn't resist the terrified gasp that escaped my lips as

I lifted it out of my pocket. It was a severed hand dripping with blood. I put it straight back.

Although I was surrounded by other people, it seemed that no-one had seen me. The person behind me just nudged past, turning round to give me a baleful look, but nothing more. His fish-like face had an expression that might have said: "So you found a severed hand in your pocket; big deal. You won't be the first, and you certainly won't be the last." But maybe it was more likely: "Get your arse out of the way, you skinny retard."

What I should have done was to turn right back and head straight to the nearest police station, but my policophobia proved to be too overwhelming. Besides, how does one walk into a police station, produce a severed hand, and expect not to get locked up right there on the spot?

I decided it was better not to stop. I'd have to deal with it after my date with Mr X. I didn't put my hand in my pocket again as I stumbled my way towards *The Hallam Cuisine*.

There was no sign of the man anywhere around the restaurant. He couldn't have been in there at all because there was a blue tape across the entrance and a couple of police officers who warded off curious onlookers milling around the place.

I sleepwalked all the way to the YMCA in Lewisham where I was lodged for the past two weeks. My head pounded, and a familiar dull pain spread through my chest, a sensation of concentrated gloom that has become my close companion over the past couple of years. At the worst of times, it felt like a jagged rip in the heart - a yawning chasm that emitted nothing but despair and despondence. It hurt like an internal damage that oozed with blood and bile, occasionally climbing up my gullet and overwhelming my taste buds. My life was a dreary routine, a fool's errand, a futile journey, a lost course and a dog's dream.

I'd got it all wrong for far too long.

Perhaps the old man was right after all. What was the point in keeping to the law when life in prison would be paradise compared to living on the cold and lonely streets? Three square meals, to say the least, and there would be structure and order - no need to look for work or keep up unnecessary pretexts of good behaviour. My freedom was a pointless, unsustainable burden.

I lost track of time and everything else, and I almost walked past the hostel. There was no-one in the communal lounge as I entered. I sat numbly in front of the old TV and stared at the photofit flickering on the screen. The grim voice of a news presenter was announcing the murder of a waitress at a restaurant. She'd been seen having an argument with a stalker two weeks before. The image on the screen didn't do justice to my rugged, handsome features. My forehead wasn't as large, and those eyes were too far apart.

I didn't have long to wait.

A sudden stampede of boots outside, and then the crash of police ramming the door off its hinges, even though it wasn't necessary. I didn't make any fuss as I was led away, still wearing the jacket with the dead girl's hand in its pocket.

He Didn't Return Home that Night

At 12 pm on Friday, Daniel abruptly stood up from his desk and headed for the door. "I'm having an early lunch today," he declared, "plus, I've got a little errand to attend to. I'll be back in an hour."

Nelson eyed him uneasily over his gold-rimmed D&G spectacles. "I want that proposal on my desk before 5 pm. Any slip up on this one, we'll all be out of work before the end of this month." From the look in his eye, Daniel could tell he wasn't joking.

"It's all covered, Nel. I'll be putting in the final touches as soon as I'm back. I'll make that thirty minutes instead of an hour."

Where the hell was Delis? When Sergeant James found that Delis was to take over from him that day, he'd called her to say that he had to leave the post no later than 7 pm for his and Laura's 12th anniversary dinner at *Chapmans'*. Delis had assured him that she'd be there on time. Although she was a nonchalant young officer who got away with far too much because of her blonde hair and youthful charm, she normally kept her word.

It wasn't until 7:10 pm that the front door finally burst open. But it wasn't Sergeant Delis. It was a pregnant woman in her mid-thirties. She was small and slim, and she carried herself with some style, despite her six-month bump. Her face was pale and tight, and she looked around nervously as she approached.

"Is there a female officer on duty?" she asked.

"If you must be seen to by a female officer, then perhaps you'd better wait for my colleague, who should be here shortly."

Whatever it was that warranted the exclusive attention of a female officer, he'd rather not be involved; best to let Delis come and deal with it. But twenty minutes passed, and there still was no sign of Sergeant Hilton. The pregnant woman fidgeted on the hardback chair in the small reception room. Her hands and feet became increasingly agitated, and her face stretched into a curious ghostlike appearance.

James, now resigning himself to the worst, put a call through to Laura to say he might be late. He squeezed his eyes shut and braced himself in anticipation of the inevitable barrage that was sure to erupt from the other end of the line.

When he'd recovered sufficiently, he turned to the woman. "Any particular reason why you want to talk to a female police officer?"

"I've come to report that my husband has gone missing."

Hmm… another missing husband, James thought. "Tell me about your husband; is he ill, disabled or with any limiting conditions?"

"He's not disabled or anything. He went to work, and he's not been back for three days."

James was doodling on a small piece of paper on the table. Husbands disappeared all the time, only to re-appear in the bosom of other women.

"How come you're only just reporting it, if he's been missing for three days?"

"I didn't know until this evening."

Sergeant James frowned.

"I was away at my sister's in Birmingham for three days. I called his mobile and it kept going to his voice mail. I thought he hadn't bothered to charge it; he's always forgetting…"

"So what makes you think he's been missing for three days if you, yourself, have been away? He could have been home during the time."

"No, he's not been home since Friday. He didn't go back home that night. His lasagne is still in the microwave where I put it, and the bed has not been slept in. When I called his work, I found they haven't seen him there today."

"Okay," James said, pulling the computer keyboard closer, "I'll take down some details and log an initial missing persons report in our database, but my main feeling here is that there is nothing to be worried about."

Daniel's rendezvous with Mandy was in front of the *D'Alberto* bookshop in Covent Garden. It took him only twenty minutes - a fifteen-minute tube ride and a brisk walk from Leicester Square station. He'd already built up a mental picture from Mandy's voice when she called his mobile earlier that morning. He put her down as a mousy blonde in her early to late twenties with the physique of an air hostess. "Daniel Tusons?" she'd said, in a voice he initially thought to be a child's, "I have some information of serious interest to you." She didn't pause to give him any chance to recover. "It will be to your best advantage if you meet me before the information gets into other hands." It sounded like a well-practised recital, and it left Daniel in no doubt that it was the opening gambit for a vicious blackmail squeeze.

As far as Daniel was concerned, there was only one way of dealing with blackmailers, and he knew what he had to do as soon as the opportunity presented itself and as soon as he'd ascertained that she was acting on her own. It was just a shame he had to cut short his current assignment and go back to doing underground activities with the rest of the gang. He'd hoped to settle down in his current identity for at least eight years. He was getting quite attached to Yasmeen, and looking forward to being a dad again. This assignment was supposed to be an easy one, with the perk of a long and sustained family life, until this evil cow turned up.

His mental picture was not too far off. The only thing he got wrong was her age - she was in her late thirties. Although her little blue eyes glittered, they did not light up her sullen pale face, and her mouth was rather too firm. She handed Daniel a large envelope without saying anything. He took a casual peep that told him all he needed to know. The envelope contained a set of photographs that he immediately recognized to be different wedding pictures of himself and his several brides. The pictures did not flood Daniel's mind with any happy memories.

"What do you want?" he asked finally.

"You have only four hours to find ten grand, or these pictures go first to your wife, and then to the police."

There was no point bluffing with her, Daniel thought. He'd just play along until he got his chance. He was at least partly relieved because she was only thinking of telling his wife and the police. She had no idea about his real enemies. He knew the moment he laid eyes on her that she was just some hacker who'd got hold of the data by scouring the Web and putting two and two together. "Cyberdredging" is what they call it. Well, this cyberdredger's just dredged up her own demise, he thought.

"Okay, let's say I give you ten grand, then what's to stop you from coming again for more?"

She smiled a wry smile and shrugged.

"Look, I can get you the money, you'll just have to come and pick it up from my flat, 46 Grosvenor Road in

Blackheath."

"I'll be there, 4 pm."

That was it. She'd bought it, hook, line and - most hopefully - sinker. Daniel smiled as he walked away; he knew a hundred and one ways of making a person disappear.

On Tuesday, when Sergeant James Elias arrived at the station to be assigned to his day's beat, he was surprised to find a message for him to report at the headquarters on Cannon Street immediately. He was to see Superintendent Dick Wilson, who was in charge of the district units. James could not help the sudden pang of foreboding that threatened to overwhelm him. He had no idea what to expect; he was aware of the regional restructuring and reorganization rumours swirling about in the force. At this time, a summons to the headquarters was unlikely to be for a recommendation. On the contrary, his entire unit was plagued by disincentives and de-motivation so that only a few of the officers could be considered to be performing to their best ability. Perhaps it was time to make a scapegoat out of someone, and maybe that person was him.

On reflection, though, there shouldn't have been any reason for him to be disciplined. After all, he worked long hours when it was required, even at significant personal cost. The previous day, for instance, he'd carried on working when Sergeant Delis failed to turn up. He attended to the deranged pregnant woman whose husband had gone AWOL, patching her up and sending her on her way. He didn't leave until alternative cover was arranged, which was close to 9 pm. Fortunately, he was still able to attend the dinner, and he hoped Laura believed him when he said he'd make it up to her.

In all his three years in the force, Sergeant James had only been to the headquarters twice. He quickly went to the eighth floor of the main building, where the Superintendent's office was located. The Super was a burly Scotsman in his fifties, with the gruff voice of a perpetual pipe-smoker, and one bloodshot eye.

James stood stiffly in the doorway.

"Come in, Elias," he roared. "Don't just stand there."

James went in further and was surprised to find that the same pregnant woman who had reported her husband missing was also sitting in the office. Oh dear, he thought, perhaps she'd gone there to complain about his handling of the matter. But when he looked at her, and she greeted him with a weak smile, he began to relax a little.

"Sergeant Elias, I'm officially putting you in charge of the case of the missing Mr Tusons. I want you to perform all necessary enquiries. You may call on any resource from the district pool."

"Right, sir," was all James could say. He was pleased that he'd been given his own case and was convinced that the Superintendent was testing him. If he handled this one right, who knew what it could lead to?

Mandy was a woman of many identities, which was why she didn't have any close friends. If she did, it would cause the affairs of her different personalities to overlap, and that could lead to massive problems. She'd managed so far without a hitch, but all that was about to change.

At the hairdresser's, she had bumped into Yasmeen, her long-lost childhood friend from way back when she was in secondary school in Birmingham - the only real friend she still remembered with any kind of fondness. They'd both been shocked to see each other. Mandy hadn't changed too drastically. She was a straightforward adult version of her old self - still blonde and still slim. Her face was harder, though, and her eyes had acquired a certain forbidding lustre. She was obviously still single and would probably never settle down into family life. Yas, on the other hand, was still soft and vulnerable. She was married and obviously pregnant.

After they'd exchanged the usual pleasantries and reminiscences, they swapped contact details and parted ways, and that was that. But the reunion had rekindled a sense of camaraderie that Mandy had not felt for a long time. She suddenly remembered what it was like to have a friend you could confide in without any reservations. She'd found herself thinking about Yasmeen at work. She even used the police online enquiry system to see if she could find anything on Yasmeen. That was when she stumbled on the activities of Daniel, Yasmeen's husband. She decided that the best thing to do was to warn her friend about the situation, so they met at the *Costa*

Café on Hogarth Street.

"Some awful news about your 'Mr Charming', I'm afraid."

"What? Has he been having an affair? I wouldn't put it past him, really."

"Well, it's worse than that. You won't like it at all."

"What is it, then? Please don't keep me guessing."

"Your Daniel is an identity thief with a history of..." Mandy cleared her throat for effect. She was surprised how coolly Yasmeen was taking all this so far. She'd always been a tough person with a deceptively vulnerable exterior; she should have been the one in the police force.

"A history of what?"

"...serial bigamy. He has a wife in Scotland, Spain and France. You, my dear Yasmeen, are wife number four."

Yasmeen's eyes clouded over, and her face crumpled into a mask of anger and despair. "No, that's not true. It can't be true."

"Sorry Yas, I can show you wedding photos and documents."

"But how did you know this? Where did you get it from?"

"Benefits of working with the police, I guess." Mandy held her friend's hand. "I know this must be extremely difficult for you at the moment, but if I were in your position, I'd see what I could get out of this before turning him over to the law."

"How could I do that?" she sobbed.

It could have been a lament, or recoil from the malice in Mandy's suggestion, but Mandy took it to be a cry for revenge.

"Don't worry, I'll show you how. I'll help you to get him."

Emboldened by the confidence that the Superintendent had placed in him, Sergeant James Elias mapped out his course of action for tackling the case of the missing Mr Tusons. He'd looked over the details and concluded that the answer was in the missing man's place of work. That was where he spent most of his time. He would have friends there, or at least colleagues who knew him well enough.

The amicable and pretty HR manager at AMTADEK allowed him to use one of the meeting rooms to interrogate members of Daniel's team. First, he spoke with an angry Nelson Park, who thought Daniel had sold out to one of the competitors, and had deliberately sabotaged the bid that he was supposed to be the chief negotiator of. Instead, Nelson had to blunder his way through a presentation that he'd hastily thrown together on Monday after Daniel failed to turn up. He was convinced that the bid was as good as lost.

"He won't even answer his mobile phone," Nelson lamented.

"It's quite serious, since even his wife hasn't seen or heard from him either," Sergeant James said, which caused the angry man to soften up a little. "Did you notice anything different about him that day?"

"Well, he seemed a bit distracted. I think he took a call on his mobile earlier, around 9:30 am."

"Does he have any close friends here, or any colleague he spends time with?"

"No, Daniel was a one-man show. He was not close to anyone. He made no conversation outside work matters. He doesn't get involved in the mundane banter that goes on in the office either."

"What about enemies? Has he had a run-in with anyone here?"

"Not that I'm aware of. As I told you, the man keeps to himself."

James questioned two others from Daniel's team, but he didn't unearth anything of real significance.

Now he was convinced that whatever happened to Daniel had nothing to do with his workmates, but it might still have something to do with the company, since that was where he was last seen. He wondered whether Daniel was involved in selling company information to competitors, or if he was a plant in the company.

There was one more place James decided to check later that day, although he didn't expect to find any real leads there, since the man's wife had said that he hadn't returned to the flat. There was always a chance that he might stumble on some diary, letter or note with some vital information.

James was on his way when a call came through from Cherry Clayton at the HQ, who was running a check on Mr Tusons' CV, which he'd earlier faxed to the headquarters.

"Just want you to know we're not dealing with an ordinary person here. Daniel Tusons is an extremely dangerous criminal with links to the *Vorovski Mir* - a formidable Russian gang whose name literally means 'World of thieves'. He's been floating around under various guises for more than fifteen years, using marriages to unsuspecting women to support a false identity."

"Thanks for the heads up," James replied, beginning to wonder whether he wasn't already out of his depth. This new piece of information changed everything.

"One more thing," said Cherry from the other end of the line, "There is a marker in the database logs saying that the records have also been accessed last week by another officer from your district."

James was puzzled. "Who was that?"

"Sergeant Delis Hilton."

Mandy parked her Ford Escort two streets away from Grosvenor Road. A brief look at her digital wristwatch told her that it was 15:50. She'd set some time aside to carry out a precautionary check of the Tusons' ground floor flat. She patted the .45 Glock 30 in the hip pocket of her stretch jeans. She'd never used it outside training, but she knew that if she had to, she could do so without hesitation. This Tusons guy could try to be troublesome, especially because he was dealing with a woman. However, she knew he had the cash ready - or at least some cash - because she'd tailed him after they parted. He'd been into the NatWest bank on Wallpole High Street, where he spent a considerable amount of time, and then he'd been in the Barclays three doors down the street. She hoped that, for his own sake, he wasn't going to try anything stupid.

Standing against the bedroom wall, Daniel looked down the street through the slightly parted blinds. He stiffened when the slim, blonde figure slid into view. She walked stealthily, like an amateur bullfighter, glancing round and taking in the details of the neighbourhood. If she was trying to make sure that nobody had seen her coming towards the flat, then that was excellent because, sure as hell, nobody was going to see her come out either. He saw the bulge in her hip pocket and smiled mirthlessly. Then he made his way to the front door to welcome his guest.

The moment Sergeant James Elias entered the flat he knew that something was amiss. He was immediately on his guard when he noticed the tidiness of the place. He hadn't imagined Mrs Tusons as a cleaning freak, especially in her pregnant condition.

James shared out the rooms among his assistants, PC Wallace and PC Terry, for detailed inspection. He stayed in the lounge, initially flicking through the magazines on the centre table for any clues. Now he was extremely concerned about Sergeant Hilton. He'd earlier called to the police post at Hextable to check if anyone had heard from her. The last time she was seen around the police station was Thursday, when she called in briefly and left in a rush, which was typical of her. At the time, she appeared to have another woman in her car, who matched the description of Mrs Tusons. James now thought he had at least some idea what might have happened. But what puzzled him was why Sergeant Delis had not gone through the correct procedure and involved her colleagues in whatever she'd found on Daniel Tusons. Did she share some sort of history with him?

He tried to contact Mrs Tusons, who had gone back to her sister in Birmingham. When he found that he was getting nowhere, he arranged with Birmingham police to have her brought back to London for questioning. He didn't clear it with the Superintendent, and he hoped it wasn't the wrong move.

"Boss, come and see this." The urgency in PC Wallace's voice caused James to snap to attention. Wallace had gone through the back door of the kitchen and was looking into the window of what appeared to be a small garden shed.

"I think there's a body in there."

Terry slammed into the shed door with his shoulder, and it gave with a loud creak and the sound of splintering timber. "Christ!" he exclaimed as he stepped inside. "It's Daniel Tusons, alright."

He was lying there in the middle of the shed, among a pile of cardboard boxes, parts of what looked like a damaged tricycle, pieces of polystyrene foam and broken glass. He had a hole in his forehead, and his eyes were staring up at the ceiling.

Mandy didn't even make it to the door of Daniel's flat. In spite of her meticulous reconnaissance, she hadn't reckoned on the involvement of a third party; hence she hadn't detected the presence of the black Audi Q5 parked only two streets away.

It all happened far too quickly for her to react with any sort of defence. The car screeched to a stop halfway between her and the flat, the front passenger door swung open, and the unmistakable barrel of a Smith & Wesson motioned for her to get in at once. It was dark in the car, and the front seats were separated from the passenger area by a finely-perforated screen. Mandy's heart pounded in her ears as the long, muscular arm of the driver shot out and pulled the door shut after her.

"Who the hell are you and what do you want from me?" she demanded as she tried to regain her breath. By this time, the car had sped up Grosvenor Avenue and turned on to the main road. Her captor did not respond. Instead, he stared stonily ahead, his pale face twitching intermittently. He had a full head of jet black hair, and his gleaming eyes were stained with a dash of yellow and red. Mandy thought he had eastern European features. She still had her gun in her pocket, but she was sure that this man was aware of her every move. Besides, she didn't know who, or what, was in the back of the car, behind the screen.

"Look," she tried once more, "I'm a police officer on

undercover duty. If you don't let me go at once, you'll find yourself in very serious trouble."

"I'm a policeman too."

The gruff voice that came from behind the screen caused Mandy to catch her breath.

"The only person who is in trouble at this moment is you," the voice continued.

She could hardly believe her ears, yet there could be no mistaking that voice.

"Super! What... What the hell is happening? What are you doing here?"

"Shut up, Hilton!" Superintendent Wilson snapped at her. "You're in no position to be asking any silly questions. Not after you have just compromised a very important operation."

Mandy's mind was whirling crazily as she searched desperately for some remotely credible story. There was no point carrying on with the undercover pretext; the Super would be aware of all the current cases in progress.

"You don't even have any idea of the size of the trouble you're in. We've been tailing your man for the past two weeks in the hope that he'll lead us to Cougar, but thanks to your blackmailing blunder..."

"I'm sorry," she sniffed. Her mind was still working feverishly to make sense of the whole thing. If such an operation was going on, then why hadn't they warned her off as soon as she'd strayed into the picture? Why was the Super dealing with this personally? And what the hell was he doing in this screened vehicle, driven by this thuggish-looking bloke? It all led to the strong like-lihood that "big boss" was into something dark and dodgy, which did not augur too well for her at the moment, either.

"But, sir, is this an official police investigation?"

"You just keep your pretty mouth shut, or you'll be in even bigger trouble. Anyway, you'll be pulling it with the rest of my crew when you come back out of hiding. Your friend Yasmeen is with us too. I'm surprised even you had been fooled by her fake pregnancy. Well, she even managed to fool her so-called husband."

"What... Yasmeen? You mean she's not..." Mandy faltered, reeling as if she'd just been slapped very hard on the face. She could never have imagined Yasmeen being part of such a setup and regretted that she'd been taken in by her deception.

"C'mon, girl, hand over that pea shooter before somebody gets hurt," his curt voice rasped, and his gloved hand reached out through a slit in the screen and snatched the gun from her limp sweaty hand.

"You're going on a long trip for a while, and then you'll be working with us. Either that or you'll have to face charges for Daniel Tusons' murder. Take your pick."

"Murder...? But..." she stuttered, "he's not -"

"He'll soon be. And there'll be no doubt in the mind of that schmuck I put in charge of the case who the killer is."

His voice trailed off in a cough that ended in some-thing that sounded like a chuckle.

All that Glitters

I loitered around the corridor of the Applied Science Department on the fifth floor of the Science Faculty building, within view of the entrance to lab 7A, keeping a heavily mascaraed eye on Professor Dixon's office door. I didn't have to wait for long. A bespectacled, balding man in his late 40s, with intelligent drooping moustache, soon emerged.

"Ah! You must be one of the new intakes..." The words were delivered in a caramel drawl with a London accent. "I'm afraid you're thirty minutes too early for the tutorial."

"Oh!" I feigned surprise, fumbling with the lecture timetable which I'd taken from Janet.

"Don't worry; I like my students to be eager. You may keep me company in the laboratory while I set up my slides."

"Thanks."

The professor held the wood panelled swing door open with his free hand, and I daintily stepped into a brightly-lit hall with several tables and bar stools. He plunked the compact projector he was carrying on the large table at the front and deftly set about his task.

"We haven't been properly introduced," he intoned. "I guess you already know I'm Professor Dixon. But please, don't call me 'Prof' like the rest of the plebs round here. Call me Alan."

"I'm Veronica Jones." I deliberately kept my voice low. "First year applied." I allowed my hand to go lame in the grip of his handshake. He lingered just slightly too long.

"I can assure you a head start in this course, seeing you're such a keen student." He winked at me, and then produced a business card from his jacket pocket. "Be sure to call me if you need any sort of help." He hesitated. "Perhaps we can catch up for dinner at some point?" It was more of a question than an invitation. A speculative gambit.

I didn't reply. Instead, I smiled sweetly.

A fast worker indeed; by the end of the encounter, he'd extracted my mobile number and a promise to meet up later for dinner. I couldn't wait to tell Janet and watch her consumed with envy.

Of course, I had no intention of honouring his invitation. That was not the way to play the game. Instead, I picked up Tony DiFranco, a second-year physics geek. I'd met him in the SUB in my first week on campus. He was only too eager for an impromptu date and had no idea of the role he was about to play in the Veronica Jones mind games show.

We went to *Henryz*, just next door to the posher *Crusties* where the Prof was waiting. I snuggled close and giggled loudly as we gambolled past. Tony roared with laughter as he enjoyed his unexpected luck, which I knew wasn't going to last more than fifteen minutes. I could feel the heat of the Prof's gaze as we swept past, but I didn't turn and look.

I didn't attend any lectures for the next four days. Then on Friday, I had to meet up with Mel outside the library at 3:30 pm to give her the new *Freemans* summer catalogue. As I waited, I was startled by a familiar caramel voice.

"Ha, there you are... Standing your lecturer up like that isn't a particularly smart way to go about a successful scholarship, is it?" His rugged face loomed out of nowhere, but his benevolent expression did not match the menace of his words. Clearly, he'd only said them in jest.

"Oh, I'm sorry. I forgot," was all I could muster.

"Never mind that, Veronica. Glad I ran into you. Perhaps you can make up by coming with me to dinner at *La Grande Plaza* later tonight. I'll pick you up at 7:30 pm."

Not just anyone ate at *La Grande*. It had been *Playboy*'s featured restaurant for the last three months running. Everyone wanted to be seen entering or leaving the *Plaza*. It was the kind of place you took a girl you were desperate to impress. And you didn't go anywhere near the place if you didn't have money to burn. I'd been there before with some bloke named Martin, who was utterly besotted. He must have spent his life savings on the dinner that night. He was now probably busy fending off bailiffs and debt collectors, as I hadn't heard from him since then.

La Grande Plaza was not the sort of place you turned up in dressed in a pair of jeans and a cheap grandmother cardigan. So I put on my favourite low-cut, red, silk Freeman's number that showed my shoulders and all my other luscious assets. The simple pearl necklace and matching miniature celandine droopers were likely to have cost another fan of mine an absolute fortune. I opted for my Crocodile Birkin bag as well, because it was an instantly recognizable fashion rave, and it was just big enough for my trove of make-up accessories.

Prof arrived punctually, in his black Brioni dinner suit. He looked like an amateur artist's impression of Pierce Brosnan in *Tomorrow Never Dies*. His hair was brushed back and thrown forward at the front to accomplish a Donald Trump effect that might actually have worked if he'd had enough hair to carry it off.

He gesticulated profusely with his moustache, which seemed to have a life of its own. It gleamed in the dim, soft light, as he drawled on and on about his current work in molecular biology and cell signalling. When the waiter arrived, he ordered R. Renaudin Brut Rose L'Espiegle NV. He confidently assured me that I'd soon see why it was his favourite wine. Suddenly, I heard a familiar voice, and turned round to see a couple walking past. The man was Marcus Mathews, the charismatic TV presenter whose fame was benefiting from a recent extramarital scandal. The Prof waved in their direction, and they waved back.

Another gentleman stopped by as well, and pumped the Prof vigorously by the hand. When he cast a wooden bow in my direction, I smiled and inclined my head in acknowledgement. He and the Prof chatted sundries for a while, and he was soon on his way.

"That's Ed Kyritz," said the Prof, as the man disappeared up the ornate flight of stairs to the left of the main entrance. "He owns the restaurant." I recognized the name, of course. I'd just never seen him in person.

I opened my Birkin and fiddled about with my base foundation compact while he went on about the jazz group softly jamming in the background. The current music was an adaptation of Roberto Solero's new rap mix with 50 Cent. Then he switched the conversation to hip-hop, R 'n' B and garage. I thought that for a man of his generation he had a surprising grasp of contemporary youth music.

We were halfway through the main course - lobster thermidor for me and venison with port and redcurrant sauce for him - when he suddenly fixed me with a curious gaze. "Well, Veronica, I've been doing all the talking this evening. Tell me about yourself."

It was the worst question anyone could have asked me. It was like handing you a rifle and saying, "Go on and shoot yourself." But it wasn't a problem I couldn't handle. I'd got my story about my adoptive rich parents and my dynastic Chinese roots nicely polished for the occasion. I was used to the unspeakable luxury of an incredibly wealthy household, one from which I had to flee for the sake of my own sanity. Also I'd turned down Cambridge for a less distinguished university because I wanted to live in a real world and mix with real people.

He listened, with his head resting against a clenched fist and his right elbow supported by the table. His dark grey eyes were a mesmerizing pool of deep concentration and perfect attention.

When I finished my well-rehearsed presentation, he said, "Yes, I know what you mean by breaking free from the manacles of indulgence. I had a similar upbringing. I've enjoyed working with underprivileged people on whom I've had a significant impact."

He smiled and began to examine his sparkling platinum cuff links, which were in the shape of a crown. The dinner would have been absolutely perfect if the Professor hadn't ruined it when, once loosened up by the wine, he rambled on about his vintage cars, his yachts and his numerous luxury apartments scattered throughout London and Paris. Then he boasted about his connections. "I'm on first-name terms with the most powerful people in the world. The second most senior police officer in the UK, Sir Alex Dixon...Well, he's my brother."

He was on the government's science advisory think-tank, and he received holiday season's greetings from Buckingham Palace every year without fail.

Okay, so the guy was super rich, and he had serious connections. Was I supposed to be impressed? I lost my appetite at once and opted to skip dessert. We both had coffee to finish while his moustache twitched. A curious expression then came over his face. I'd seen that look before, and I knew that when you saw it on a man's face, he was either about to propose for your hand in marriage or about to break wind.

"So what about us?"

I busied myself reapplying my makeup, closely inspecting my face in my compact mirror glass. Exactly what kind of 'us' was he talking about here? Was it a long-term 'us' or an 'us' that would only last for one night? I wondered how many 'usses' he had on the go. How did all his 'usses' stack up? Was my own 'us' bigger than poor old Mrs Dixon's?

When would this old Prof eventually run out of 'usses'?

I was spared from having to answer his question when his smart phone squealed, and he quickly picked it up. His frown deepened as he listened and muttered intermittently in response. Finally, he said, "Okay, I'd better be on my way then," in a voice laden with resigned irritation.

"Sorry, dear. Apparently, I've been having so much fun tonight that I forgot a crucial appointment. I'll drop you back at the halls."

As we approached the car, he asked, "How come you didn't tell me about your accommodation issue?" That certainly took me by surprise. I wondered who he'd been talking to.

I experienced a minor panic. The last thing I wanted was for him to poke around and get involved in administrative matters on my behalf. But as it turned out, he had something entirely different in mind. "I did tell you I own some apartments. There's one you can use if you want to. It's not exactly student accommodation, but it's a roof over your head, and it's only a few tube stops from the campus."

I was impressed by the offer, but I was sure it was not altogether altruistic. "I couldn't possibly..." I protested lamely.

"Don't worry. It's not occupied at the moment, and I just hate to see it stay vacant." He handed me a set of keys on a leather key ring. "34C Justin Court, just off Grosvenor Street. Only five minutes' walk from St James's Park tube station."

He was right when he said it was not an ideal student accommodation. It was more like a top-of-the-range crib for a high-flying city worker with a six-figure salary, a fat cat bonus and a playboy lifestyle. There was a manned entrance with a concierge in a smart blue uniform, who nodded respectfully as I went in. The lift car was perfumed, and the walls were all lined with spotless mirrors. The corridor on the third floor led to flat 34C, which overlooked a finely-tended courtyard with an elegant marble water feature right at the centre - the statue of a Greek goddess with water cascading from its head down to white crystal pebbles at its feet. The double doors to the flat were crafted from some heavy, dark wood, inset with gleaming chromium bars. The handle was a precision component with a counterweight hydraulic lever that could only have been designed by an aeronautics engineer.

The smell of leather and potpourri greeted me as I entered. The floor was covered wall to wall with a soft cream shaggy rug. The first room was the lounge, and it was a fair size. A glass stool in the centre supported an exotic Persian flower vase. There were three other doors, two opposite the main entrance and one at the side that led to a full-featured kitchen with shiny brown work-tops, an electric cooker and an oversized American-style refrigerator-freezer.

Another door led to a tastefully-furnished bathroom and still one more to a bedroom fit only for a princess. The flat had almost everything I could want. Only one thing was missing - a party. So, without any undue prevarication, I contacted Tim Guthrie. If anyone could conjure a party in a hurry, he was the guy. I rang Janet and Spotty Alexa, and the drinks were sorted. If the fairy godmother thought her magic wand was cool, that's because she never knew about the Apple iPhone 4S.

The first guests arrived at 9 pm: two guys in leather jackets and jeans. I'd never seen them before. They came because they'd heard there was a party. In the space of thirty minutes, the whole place was heaving. Tim brought his MC kit and disco lights and transformed the lounge into an awesome dance arena.

It was one of the most spectacular parties I'd ever thrown. It went on until 2 am, when the neighbours had finally had enough and called the police.

When the police arrived, they were surprisingly relaxed about the whole situation. Despite the heady stench of marijuana and syringes and needles everywhere, no-one was arrested. The police were only interested in moving the troublemakers out with the least possible fuss.

I woke up around 11 am the following day. There was no sign of Janet, who had stayed behind after everyone else left. She had a mid-semester assessment test at 9 am. I was glad I didn't have to sit for an exam after the sort of night we'd just had. My ears still buzzed and my head hurt like hell.

But when I saw the amount of damage that had taken place, my head cleared at once. The whole place had been trashed. The paintings on the wall were all ripped. Where the wallpaper had not been scratched, there were filthy stains all the way up to the ceiling.

The whole place reeked of stale beer and vomit.

The kitchen door had been taken off its hinges. I tiptoed warily on the slippery floor and surveyed the unwholesome mess of pizza, cigarette butts and multi-coloured pills on the worktop. The fridge door hung open at a jaunty angle, and I knew it would never close properly again. I wasn't brave enough to look in the bathroom. My immediate impulse was to flee. There was no way I was going to stick around in such a stink-hole. So I packed my bags and went back to my squat in Janet's bunker.

What was I going to tell the Prof? We'd just have to play cat and mouse until the brown smelly stuff finally hit the fan.

Every time my mobile rang, I froze with apprehension. I even grew a pair of highly sensitive antennae, and checked before I entered the library or any of the lecture rooms. He filled up my voice mail and sent several text messages which I didn't reply to.

After three days, I began to relax. He'd stopped trying to get in touch. I guessed he'd finally written me off as a rotten brat. So I was utterly unprepared when I stepped out of the library and caught sight of the Prof's Black BMW X6 parked in front of the library entrance. Without turning round, I knew he was not far behind me.

"What a delightful surprise," he said.

I recoiled. I wished I had the powers of Houdini.

"Found you just in time. We're having a departmental luncheon tomorrow for some visiting lecturers from China. I want you there as my star pupil."

What could be more exciting? I thought.

"But beforehand, what about dinner at the *Grande Plaza*, perhaps later this evening?"

"Sure."

"Pick you up 8:30." And he was gone. Quick business. All conducted like an exchange of contraband between two drug dealers. I couldn't wait to brag to the girls about another big date with the Prof.

This time we got a table by the window overlooking the street. The proprietor was even more congenial, planting a kiss on my outstretched hand while oozing charm and compliments.

The Prof didn't talk much initially, but he smiled and listened attentively when I delved into an elaborate treatise on the latest in handbags and shoes. He also loosened up a bit after a couple of glasses of rosé, and embarked on a lengthy rant about chromosomes and telomeres, laughing in places that I thought weren't even remotely funny. He had the sense of humour of a dead fish, but the thing that made me laugh was the antics of his dancing moustache.

I came to full attention when his moustache began to twitch uncontrollably. I'd come to realize it was an early warning signal for a change of topic. But I was unprepared for what he said next.

"Christ, Veronica! What happened in the apartment?" The issue had obviously been eating him up all the while during dinner. He'd just kept a lid on it and pretended that he was not bothered. "I couldn't believe my eyes. It was an utter mess! More than a mess, actually. A disaster!"

"Oh," I said, trying to speak carelessly, "We just had a little party."

"Must have been one hell of a party, that."

I shrugged. No point showing I was petrified, or for that matter, showing I was in the least remorseful. "We had a lot of fun. We did."

"Of course, you did… I guess you moved back to campus accommodations?"

I had nothing to say to that.

"Here's what we can do," he said. "Let's swap your key for Apartment 7B. Fortunately, the tenant there just left. Do go easy on the partying this time though, won't you?"

I was astounded by his reckless generosity. It was actually a shame that he wasn't going to get whatever he thought he was going to get in return for it.

He offered to drop me at the apartment, but I insisted I had to meet up with Janet to complete an overdue intermediate physiology essay.

Later that night I arrived at my new apartment. It was just as tastefully furnished as the first one. It had exquisite dark brown laminate flooring with a small square Persian rug in the middle of the lounge. The bathroom was larger and had cream-coloured wall tiles. I ran some warm water in the copious bathtub while I stared at the ornate tin ceiling tiles and wondered how long this ride was going to last. I could feel a sense of guilt coming on. Anytime I felt guilty, it was always William Cheng's voice I heard.

Go away, William. I won't let you ruin the party with your pathetic whining.

I shut my eyes and savoured the light touch of the foam bath and the soothing warm water. Thirty minutes passed, and my mobile began to ring. I let it go on until it stopped, but it soon started ringing again. Some people never gave up, and I couldn't care less. Still, it was reassuring to know that some smitten lover boy of mine was desperate to make contact.

The following three days were filled with meticulous schemes for avoiding the Prof. He sent an army of text messages and voice mails, none of which I ever reciprocated. The concierge presented me with a massive bouquet, with a note from the Prof, on my arrival from a particularly late outing. The concierge remarked that in all of his twenty-five years of service, it was the biggest, most beautiful bouquet he'd ever had the pleasure of delivering, and he offered to carry it to my flat.

In the days that followed, apart from the massive bouquet of flowers, I was pelted with an onslaught of expensive gifts that included designer perfumes, a Harrods voucher, a pair of alligator boots, an Emporio Armani watch, a couple of leather handbags, and an ivory manicure set. And more messages and gifts kept coming. It appeared my Prof had embarked on an expensive strategy of wearing me down with volleys of gifts, but the effect was not a sudden, overwhelming desire to jump into bed with him. Rather, it was a growing sense of guilt. William Cheng's voice raged in my head until I was about to scream.

But I had no intention of giving in. The game was never won by giving in at the slightest twinge of conscience. Prof Alan Dixon was not the first, and he was not going to be the last. There was Dr Richard, from the University of Leicester, who had been equally besotted. He was not as wealthy, but was just as generous within the limits of his widow's mite (if over £5000 worth of gifts and flowers could be regarded as such). The Dr Richard gravy train rolled on for more than two months before I decided to put him out of his misery in a spectacular fashion. From the moment he'd set his eyes on me in the auditorium, he'd turned into a fawning poodle. His weak, beady eyes twinkled, and his fat sweaty nose flared as he gushed and fawned all around me.

He put me up at the *Meridian Hotel* at £400 a night but never made any bold advances or explicit demands. He was too decent for that - initially, at least.

I'd met Dr Richard's daughter, Henrietta Richard, at the SUB, and we were getting along before I met her father. It all started with minor flirtations, some odd, slitty-eye winks and seemingly innocent touching. And then came the hand holding and snuggling together, like a pair of Siamese kittens. The whole lesbian thing was not my cup of tea, but the silly girl had got it into her pretty little head that we ought to be more than soul mates, and she was getting alarmingly amorous.

After I'd been carrying on with Henrietta and living off her dad's incredible generosity - of which she absolutely had no clue - I finally decided it was time to stage a cleverly-hatched showdown. It was time to bring Henrietta and her daddy face to face in a once-in-a-lifetime drama event.

When I finally acceded to Dr Richard's subtle but relentless overtures, he was overjoyed beyond imagination. His fawning made me feel physically ill. I told him to meet me at the hotel room and promised there would be no disappearing acts or feigned lapses of memory this time. I'd switched on my most seductive voice and told him I was going to be there, waiting, and it would be a day he'd never forget.

Henrietta was even more excited than her father when I told her I'd found a place where we could be alone together to spend some long overdue quality time. Her shrill giggle rang in my ears like the whining of a dog on heat.

She arrived ten minutes before her father, which was spot on with my plan. She was wearing her favourite large white T-shirt with a pink motif of two interlocking key symbols. Smiling coyly, she fidgeted, playing with her short, spiky hair to give her restless fingers something to do.

"Come in at once! You have no idea how much I want you," I baited.

She was frantic. Her white T-shirt was discarded without delay, and even as we thrashed about on the bed, disentangling ourselves from our clothing, I heard footsteps approaching the door, intentionally left ajar by me. A shadow was cast on the floor, and I turned with my penis in full tumescence, pointing at the horrified intruder like an accusing finger.

That was when Henrietta saw it too - my penis, that is. She emitted a petrified cry which she stopped abruptly when she saw who was at the door. Dr Richard dropped the flowers he was carrying. I wondered what shocked him more, that his object of infatuation was a girl with a penis, or that he'd caught his beloved daughter in bed with another girl. Whichever it was, the experience had certainly knocked out his usual self-assured eloquence and turned him into a goofy statue.

Henrietta threw on her clothes and bolted out of the room. Her father hesitated briefly and then lumbered after her like a zombie. That was the last I saw of either of them. For a long time, I amused myself with the thought of what they would have said to each other in the car on their way back home that night.

I'd made the transition from the pathetic, smarmy William Cheng to the gorgeous princess of fun at the age of 22. Before then in was a dreary, miserable life of rejection and self-loathing. I had my first course of oestrogen at 18 after I'd run away from my mum in Slough. I also had some reconstructions, but I held on to one little detail which I'd since christened 'William'. It was my final connection with William Cheng.

Since my transformation, I'd become everything that William could never have hoped to be. I was always doing doctors and professors. There wasn't ever going to be a shortage of them. I did have one architect in 2007. His name was Jeremy Philip, and he was quite a pillar of society in Slough. He was on the Board of the Institute of Commerce and the chairman of the Berkshire Philanthropic Guild. He parted with more than £10,000 in cash or kind over three weeks before I finally showed him William. As always, the reaction was to turn into an awestruck moron, lose total power of speech and slither away, never to appear again. It gave me such a perversely delicious sense of power to be able to inflict such a wicked mischief on men.

I was playing the game the way it ought to be played. No matter how much they pined, I'd bring it to a close only in my own time and on my own terms. But this time it was a bit different. There was too much pity, too much guilt, too much William Cheng. This guy had put me up in an extravagant apartment, bought me expensive gifts and flowers, and he'd spent a stupendous fortune on me. He'd been exceedingly polite and had not directly demanded anything in return, never alluded to his obvious intentions, and he hadn't shown any signs of frustration despite my evasiveness. His only response was to shower me with a steady downpour of generosity. It was starting to get to me. I finally resolved to set him free.

The next time he called, I was ready.

"Wow! I got through!" There was an unusual stutter. "I - I was preparing to leave a message on your voice mail as usual."

"I miss you," I said in my sweetest possible Marilyn Monroe voice. "Could you pretty please come to the apartment?"

"What? You mean, like, now?"

He got there in twenty minutes. He must have used a helicopter and walked through walls. He had on a dark brown suit and white shirt. His brow glistened with sweat, and he was slightly out of breath. He'd even managed to grab a modest bouquet and a bottle of Bollinger on his way.

"Come here, you," I growled as he put down the flowers and champagne on the centre table. He stood obediently still as I undid his purple and yellow daffodil silk tie. "Let me show you something sexy."

He held on in a gentle kiss and started to take control, his strong hairy hand stroking the back of my neck. Then he carried me to the bed, and we were soon both entwined in each other.

"Oh Veronica," he croaked as his hand slid towards my groin. He let out a startled yelp when his hand came into contact with William, and then he leapt off as if he'd touched a hot iron rod.

I watched as he staggered back. His face was a death mask of shock and bewilderment. At first his eyes widened, and then he turned an unearthly shade of grey as blood rapidly drained away from his face. He uttered a strange choking sound as if he'd been punched in the stomach. Then he slowly gathered up his trousers, picked up his coat and daffodil tie, and in a profound image of abject defeat, he slid quietly away. I couldn't suppress the delirious chuckle that tickled my throat.

That was it.

I thought I'd never hear from him again, and he'd gone the same way as the others. He'd be too ashamed to breathe a word to anyone. It was time to get myself out of the apartment and back to Janet's pad for another couple of months until the end of the semester, before moving on. Prof was a nice guy, though. But I was sent to this world to teach men - men like him - a lesson.

I called Janet to say I'd be crashing on her spare

bunk that night, but there was a certain tremulousness in her voice that I did not take too seriously at the time.

The concierge stared at me as I carried my bag across the lobby. I waved at him, but he didn't wave back. He simply turned away towards a small TV set behind the counter.

Tim Guthrie stopped me just before I reached the dorms. He rushed across the road towards me. His eyes were twinkling with excitement, and he was out of breath.

"What have you got yourself mixed up in?" he asked. "Some strange-looking guys have been asking questions about you."

"What do they want? Are they still in the premises?"

"They're questioning the guys in Wing A, including Janet. You're not in any kind of trouble, are you?"

"I don't know."

I looked around frantically, feeling more helpless and scared than ever before. "Thanks for telling me," I stuttered as I turned back toward the main road.

There was no doubt that Prof Dixon had wasted little time in letting the law loose on me. He must have called his high-ranking police brother. What a killjoy! Why did he have to take this game all so seriously? What a spiteful bastard.

They wouldn't have to try too hard to get enough on me to put me away for a long stretch. Lying about your age and gender might not be a criminal offence, but using other people's names, their birth certificates, their passports and their credit cards was clearly against the law. It was all going jolly well until the wicked Prof set the police on my trail. It was now over for me. I took out my mobile and tapped out a text message to him. I wanted to say, "GO ROT IN HELL" but instead, I simply texted, "I'M SORRY".

I walked aimlessly on, no clue where to go next or what to do. I couldn't go home to my mum in Basildon, not since I'd sent her a nude photo of myself with William (AKA my penis) in prominent display. Just something one did in a delicious moment of defiance. It gave her the final excuse to wash her hands of me altogether. And she'd written back in crystal clear terms that she no longer wanted anything to do with me.

I didn't get far.

"Veronica Jones?" A stern, mirthless voice caused me to stop and turn round. It came from a black police uniform. Upon seeing my face, he softened his voice slightly. "We've been looking for you in connection with a series of accusations relating to impersonation and identity theft. You must come with us to Leyton police station for questioning..."

I followed him to the Skoda Estate police van parked a few metres away. It occurred to me that they must have been driving behind me for some time.

At the police station, I was asked to remain at the reception desk. It turned out that they were waiting for a female officer to carry out a body search. The burly officer at the counter could not take his eyes off me. He had that deprived look only found on the faces of near-starved laboratory mice. Two other officers came in. One whistled when he saw me, and the other younger one winked. He asked the officer at the counter what I was doing there, and then volunteered to conduct the body search but was told to get lost.

PC Sally Dunne did not appear until twenty unbearable minutes later. She'd been briefed about me. She apologized politely for the delay and took some initial information. Then she said she was sorry, but she would have to frisk me before we went into the interrogation room.

"Okay," I muttered.

"Are you pregnant?"

"No."

"Are you wearing a pacemaker or any internal metallic device for health purposes or otherwise?"

"No."

I went through the security frame, and she commenced the frisk. Her gloved hand felt strangely comforting as she patted around my shoulders, briefly cupped my breast, felt around my middle and my hips. Her face remained bland and deadpan until she patted around my groin. That's when I felt her suddenly tense up.

"Christ, what's that?"

"I'm a..."

"Fuck, why didn't you say so?" she exclaimed, stepping back and holding her hands away from her body as if they'd been contaminated with high-grade plutonium dust.

The officer at the counter gave me a funny look and then broke into an unearthly cackle. "I knew there was something dodgy about this one the moment I saw her. Come on, Sally, what are you frightened of? It won't bite."

"How the hell can you tell?" she retorted. "You go ahead and search him if you want to."

"No, not me ma'am," the officer sniggered. "You started the job, so you'd better bloody finish it."

"Follow me," Sally said curtly. Maintaining a wary distance, she led me to a floodlit room with a single table and two hardbacked chairs on opposite sides. She motioned for me to sit on the chair further away from the door, giving me a wide berth as I made my way to the chair.

"I have a ridiculously long list of charges against you from across the country. It seems you've been going around universities and colleges posing as a student under different names."

I had nothing to say.

Obviously I was sure a comprehensive dossier had been rapidly put together as a matter of top priority. There was nothing that couldn't be achieved if you pressed the right buttons with the powers that be, and I was sure that was what the Prof's brother had done. No stone had been left unturned in investigating all my activities for the past ten years.

"Janice Trent, psychology, at the University of Surrey; Miranda McDonald, literature and drama,

Portsmouth College; Sue Collins, maths, Leeds; Sharon Davies, biochemistry, Exeter; Liz Martins, history major, Birmingham... We found twenty-six student ID cards in your possession."

I felt a strange lump of remorse ascend my throat. There was no way I was going to get out of this one.

"If you have no answer to the charges, I'm afraid we have to keep you here for the time being. Is there someone you want us to contact and inform of your whereabouts, so they could arrange legal and bail?"

"I have no-one."

PC Sally glared balefully at me. There wasn't a hint of pity in her cold grey eyes. "In that case, I have no choice but to keep you here," she said flatly.

An alarming chill came over me. I couldn't afford to be separated from my make-up and HRT kit for long. The consequences were not worth thinking about.

All sense of time vanished while I was detained in the Leyton police solitary cell, and all my worst fears were realized. The place had no windows, and the lights were left on all the time. It was a small, bare, square room with a bed built into the wall, a well-used WC and a grime- covered wash basin with a single cold water tap that was hard to turn. A faint, noisome smell hung persistently in the air, a smell I would do everything to avoid once I was out of this mess. Food was passed through a hatch at the bottom of the steel door. Another smaller hatch, at about waist level, popped open at random intervals, and a pair of eyes peered in to see what I was up to.

That was the lowest point in my life. There was nothing to do except wallow in anger and regret. Perhaps I should have got rid of William altogether. But I couldn't let go; he was my soul and my conscience.

Whenever I touched my upper lip and my chin, I felt the sharp scraping bristle of my growing moustache and beard. I must have looked an utter mess. I felt my chest and knew that my breasts had all but disappeared.

I'd turned back into William Cheng.

If I ever got out, I'd start over from the beginning. I'd take a degree in psychology and get a decent job, and then I'd hire someone to fix the Prof.

The PC who let me out of the cell was the same guy who was at the counter in reception on the day I arrived. Now that it was obvious what I was, they no longer needed PC Sally to attend to me.

"You should see yourself, mate," the police officer sniggered.

I had no aggression left in me; certainly not enough to answer him with an appropriate insult, so I just followed obediently.

"Well, the good news is there's someone here to see you."

"Who?"

I couldn't imagine. Perhaps Janet had contacted someone to find out where I was, I wondered vaguely.

I heard his voice before I saw him. It was the first time I'd seen him without his suit, except for the night in the apartment, of course.

"Jesus!" he exclaimed. "What happened to you?"

Yes, I'd been in there for three days and grown a beard, but it didn't mean I'd turned into Jesus. I knew I'd wronged the Prof, but I thought I'd suffered enough for it, and it wasn't necessary for him to turn up to gloat. My mouth was dry. All I could do was to remain tongue-tied and keep my head bowed.

"I came the moment I heard you were in trouble. A lecturer at the University of Leicester hired a private investigator to probe your activities. I wondered what you'd done to upset him."

"What? So it wasn't you?"

"Dear, surely not! Do you know a Dr Richard?"

"Oh."

"Well, I've had a little confab with him, and we've both come to a common agreement, so he's abandoned his comprehensive agenda of revenge."

"What about - "

"I've also sorted out your bail with the police. I'm hoping this misunderstanding will be resolved quickly."

"I'm so sorry..." I started to sob.

"Don't worry, Veronica, it's okay." Then he added, "You can stay at the apartment for as long as you want."

I stared at him through tear-stung eyes, unable to comprehend his generosity.

He smiled. "Look, I'll give you a lift back to the flat. I expect you'll want to sort yourself out and, of course, you must be hungry. If you want, I'll come back later and take you out for dinner?"

"Thanks, Alan," I whimpered into the offered

handkerchief, dazed by his extraordinary kindness which only made me feel more miserable.

He picked up my Birkin bag from the counter, and I followed him lamely to his BMW, parked by the main entrance.

He held the door, and I clambered into the leather upholstered seat feeling like a duckling rescued from an oil slick. My knees knocked, and I shivered from the evening breeze. Then I caught a reflection of myself in the side mirror. I flinched and burst into tears.

The Prof held my hands. "Hey, Veronica. Cheer up. A few days' rest and you'll be as good as new."

I forced myself to look into his enquiring eyes, and he smiled. "Trust me," he said, then added, "I just want you to know that I'm not doing all this out of pity. Despite everything, I still have feelings for you."

It was the last thing I expected to hear from him. I remembered how he'd reacted in the flat after the encounter.

"You're kidding, right? I don't imagine you'll want anything to do with me now."

"That's not true, honey. We're soul mates. There's no-one I'd rather be with."

"What - what about Mrs Dixon?"

"Where did you get the idea? There's never been any Mrs Dixon."

"Huh...?"

I was still trying to digest that piece of unexpected information when he did something that took me entirely by surprise. In a voice so unlike his normal baritone drawl - in a perfect soprano voice - he said, "Well, you're not the only one who's been keeping a secret." He stroked my hair and smiled, "I've not always been Alan. I started out as Cindy. I had my first transgender op when I was 16."

My mind was in a whirl. *This is not happening!*

"What - you mean …"

"So, see why we'll be good together?" he said, reaching out for my hand.

That was when I began to scream.

Once Upon a Time Bomb

When trouble finally arrived, I didn't recognize it immediately. Up until then, I'd lived a bland life. I simply gawked at other people's tales of adventure, admiring and envying their audacity at the same time.

This day, I was in my usual haunt; that rambling old pub in Woking called *The Dragon's Toenail*, counselling my second pint of Guinness. I had one eye on the cricket match, which was playing on the wall-mounted flat screen TV, and the other eye on Pete the barman, who was polishing the tumblers. That was when the tranquillity was broken by an unusual new customer.

"What does a lady have to do to get a drink around 'ere?"

She'd stumbled into the pub like some unwilling stand-up comedian catapulted on to the stage by an impatient compere. Wearing a skimpy red blouse and a black pair of stretch jeans, she was a smallish, delicate creature. Her faded, shoulder-length, blonde hair had highlights of grey, and her thin face was bemottled with telltale patches that placed her well beyond 45. She was holding one of her high-heeled shoes and standing on the other, and her open multi-strapped leather jacket completed the impression that she had just escaped from a nearby asylum. As she teetered on one leg for a fraction of a second, I feared for her anorexic frame. She quickly regained her balance, but not her breath.

After staring petulantly at Pete for half a minute, she said again, "What does a lady have to do to get a drink in this wretched..." Waving her free hand and looking round with an expression of bewildered contempt, she finally found the word she was looking for: "...dump?"

Pete didn't take his eye off the tumbler he was polishing. His face didn't betray the slightest acknowledgement of the newcomer's presence. I guessed, in his years of experience, he'd perfected the art of putting down such unwelcome intruders. He knew that the best way to demonstrate his displeasure was to deny the aberrant female newcomer the very oxygen she needed - attention. There was now a tension in the pub, and the other two punters, seated near the pool table, were now starting to stare awkwardly.

So I called out, "Come on, Pete. Give the lady a drink, for Christ's sake."

Only then did he put some ice in a glass and serve her a Bacardi and coke, with a stare colder than the ice he chucked in.

She brought her drink over and sat on the chair next to mine. "Hi, I'm Eve." Her hand was limp and cold. "What's a fine gentleman like you doing in this bog hole?"

"I like it here," I replied. "It's a good place to hide away from all the madness in the world."

I'd been a regular customer at *The Toenail* for more than four years since I finally retired from the Wopplesdon Post Office depot, where I'd been complacently marking time for more than 27 years, languidly climbing to the position of warehouse superintendent.

"You're not from round here, I suppose?" I prompted.

"No, just passing through." Her voice had a grating quality, and the accent, which she imparted through her pinched nose, was a curious mix of Canadian and Australian.

I looked at the tiny, red, thin-strapped shoe she'd put on the floor beside her chair, but she ignored my enquiring glance.

"I'm on my way back to London from Pompey, but I'm not in a rush, so I've decided to take a random stop at the Woking train station and check out the natives. Good thing they're not all like Kid Kong over there..."

I glanced across at Pete. He glowered back at me. I wasn't surprised that he'd taken such an aversion to her. He was a down-to-earth Scotsman who believed that mature women should dress and behave their age, so I guessed he had little time for the likes of Eve.

Over the course of the next two hours, I bought her three more Bacardis and in return received an elaborate chronicle of her adventures in the clubs of north London. She was a walking Wikipedia of mundane night-time events in London, nattering away about what was hot and what was cool and the next big thing about to explode on the party scene - all of which was alien stuff to me, and to which I listened with polite interest and unwavering attention.

"You know the new Jaeger Tweeds…"

"Yes," I said automatically.

"Well, straight off the catwalk, I can get you one of those for £500."

"…If you want to party, to really, really have a good time, don't go to the West End… Go straight to *Costello's* on George Street."

"Yeah." I nodded sagely.

In those excruciating two hours, she covered fashion, partying, drinking, travelling, food, TV, exotic gardening, goldfish fattening, DIY disasters, low budget interior decoration advice, underwater appliances, slimming exercises, fertility rituals of the *Milwaukee* tribe and - last, but certainly not least - eyebrow grooming tips.

"Tonight," she said contemplatively, "there's a massive rave in one of the hardcore clubs. It'll be totally irresponsible to miss out on that."

I was still wondering what on earth "a massive rave" might entail when she said, "Come with me, big boy; it'll be fun."

Immediately snapping out of my inertia, I exclaimed, "No I can't!" I was frantically scanning my comatose brain for a plausible excuse. One didn't just take off on some foolish expedition with a frivolous stranger who'd just wandered into the pub.

"Come on, Charlie. Don't shrimp out on me now."

That's when Pete waded in. "If you know what's good for you, old chap, you'll send this little parasite on her way without any further delay."

But before I could utter a word, Eve had drawn herself up to her full height, her lack of stature fully compensated for by the contortion of her thin-lined brows and the fire in her eyes, and she was striding towards Pete with incredible menace.

Then, suddenly, perhaps realizing the futility of her intent, she stopped halfway and wagged a bony index finger at him. "Now, why don't you mind your own flippin' business? You're nothing but a miserable pond life." Then she picked up her shoe, turned on her heels and marched off. But just before she reached the door, she turned round.

"So, are you coming or what?"

Brain still not fully engaged, I got up and followed her. I didn't look at Pete, but I could feel his caustic gaze boring into the back of my head as I left.

Keeping up with Eve was not easy. For a pair of short, skinny legs on wobbly high heels, she moved really fast. At first I thought she was driven by her vitriol against Pete, but as it turned out, that was her usual pace. She hopped and skipped over imaginary hurdles and, likewise, I obediently kangarooed after her.

"Where are we going?" I asked when I finally caught up.

"We're going to paint London red and blue," she declared.

I took that to tentatively mean we'd be wandering aimlessly through the streets, stopping at pubs and clubs for a swig or two. But when she said, "I'll take you to some places in London you've never even dreamt of," I felt a minor jitter run up and down my spine. I didn't look round as we approached the train station. I was sure the passers-by and lookers-on, most of whom probably knew me, would think I'd picked up a loose woman, and I, on my part, wasn't entirely sure exactly what I'd picked up.

We boarded the 7:36 to London Waterloo, sharing the space with a weary young woman and her boisterous, snotty-nosed toddler of indeterminate sex. The toddler took one look at Eve and burst into an earsplitting wail. So we quit the carriage for the next one, through the automatic connecting doors.

From Waterloo, we hopped on the Jubilee line to Finchley Road. I was a mere follower with no idea of what to expect. But the sights in the backstreets of Camden soon filled me with amusement. There were a lot of people wandering around, often to the point that we saw the same people we'd already seen. A bunch of youths were messing about, walking backwards on the broad pavement between the shops and the main road. I felt like going with them just for the fun of it. Further ahead, there was a commotion which turned out to be due to fire in a second-hand clothing shop. The smoke billowed from the entrance and windows, and people gawked from across the road at the growing prospect of a bonfire. I could smell the smoke, which, combined with my efforts to catch up with Eve, made me think my lungs were in desperate need of fresh air. Somewhere in the distance I could hear the steadily rising wailing of a fire engine.

"Stop, Eve!" I gasped. "I can't keep up."

But Eve didn't stop; she marched on with unflinching determination, and I laboured to keep my pace and my breath.

"Get out of the way, you old fart!" Eve screamed at a busker soulfully perpetrating an atrocious, sub-karaoke quality rendition of a Bob Marley song, and polluting the already noise-saturated space with the cacophony of his accordion. He glowered back at her without interrupting his unholy racket. "Sorry mate," I apologized on her behalf while still rushing to catch up. It seemed you had to be a juggler of sorts in order to get by in such a fast-paced world - a far cry from my normal, tranquil life. I definitely wouldn't be doing this again.

There was a deafening blare of a motorcycle horn immediately followed by a volley of swearing as the rider narrowly missed a fat woman who had strayed from the pavement. I saw the whole incident, and my heart leapt in a panicked concern for the poor woman, but I couldn't hang around. I turned back just in time to see Eve disappear round the next street, where an old Asian cab driver was inspecting a busted rear wheel, his face warped into a mask of perfect gloom.

Just when I thought my legs had taken enough punishment for one day, Eve turned into a squalid alleyway between Boots and a small music store. I looked around warily, thinking it was the sort of place you could end up with a long knife in your guts if you didn't keep walking. Another turn and we came upon *The Shack*, Eve's favourite club. A thin black girl, casually smoking weed, stepped aside from the entrance to let us in, eyeing me up and down with a twisted leer.

We walked into a head-pounding pandemonium of rock music and a haze of marijuana fumes. Slippery shadows writhed on the central dance floor, which we had to pass through in order to reach the crowded bar. The rhythm of the loud music mirrored the thumping in my chest.

Eve's voice cut through the palpitating din that ruled the club, and the sweaty barperson, who had more tattoos than a Persian rug and more piercings than a cheese grater, eventually served us two glasses of an electric blue drink that tasted like turpentine. A cautious sip of the weird stuff had an unexpected calming effect. It wrapped my brain in strange comforting warmth, and everything made perfect sense.

We were surrounded by strange characters, almost in every respect like zombies. Most of them had fixed, dazed gazes and dressed in the wackiest outfits - mainly black, with chains, leather straps and silver spiked collars. It was difficult to tell their ages. But once my eyes fully adjusted to the dim lighting, it was clear that there was some sort of beauty in the gathering.

Eve was saying something. I could see her lips moving, but it took some time for the sound to catch up. She was motioning towards the bar, proposing another shot of turpentine. I shook my head to decline. My head weighed a ton, and the momentum caused my whole body to sway from side to side. She shrugged in slow motion and downed another tumbler of the wicked stuff. Her eyes glowed in their sockets like coals in a fireplace, and she began to do some strange dance movements, beckoning in my direction. Under normal conditions, I would have shaken my head vigorously at the suggestion and fled the scene. But with a tummy full of turps, and lungs steeped in fumes, the only logical action was to follow her lamely and participate in her ungainly gyration.

I was in the middle of an intricate dance move, cheered on by a couple of newly-acquired chums, when suddenly disorder broke out somewhere in the far corner of the club. Shouts rose above the ambient mayhem, and a surge of activity rippled in our direction. Suddenly, there was a sharp explosion and, although I'd only ever heard it before on TV, I knew instinctively that it was the sound of a gunshot. I could feel my heart pumping faster, and my whole body tensed up in mortal dread. My immediate thought was: *How the hell did I get myself into this?* And then the lights went out, and the place was plunged into complete darkness.

"Eve!" I yelled.

But I could not hear her among the screaming and shouting. I was bashed and jostled by desperate youths trying to get out.

There was another explosion, followed by a shower of debris from the ceiling. I could hear my own voice futilely calling out for help as I struggled with the limbs that thrashed at me in the darkness. My mind was overwhelmed with fear and regret. I shouldn't have left the *Toenail*, where everything was safe and one could never come to any harm. If I didn't come out of this mêlée unscathed, how would I explain my presence in this place to Henrietta?

"Eve!"

Still no answer. She must have been far gone by then, without any thought for me.

Above the smell of sweat, alcohol and marijuana, there was now a stronger smell of burning rubber. It was becoming increasingly overpowering and I felt like throwing up.

"Eve!" I croaked again in vain.

There was a gradually escalating crescendo of a police siren, seemingly galvanising the youths into more desperate activity. Suddenly a hand grabbed me roughly by the arm and I was dragged away over a few metres before the mysterious hand released its grip. I soon found myself wedged in a scrum of panicking youths who carried me along and, miraculously, deposited me outside the club.

"Whoo hoo!" an excited teenager shouted, with a broad smile. Apparently, in his books, that commotion from which I'd just barely escaped an encounter with death was a fitting end to a perfect party.

It was astonishing how quickly my head cleared when the chilly winter wind hit me squarely in the face. Even as my legs were swiftly carrying me away from the site of danger, I glanced around furtively for Eve. She was nowhere in sight, but I was sure she was quite capable of looking after herself.

I caught the last train at Waterloo, just before midnight, arriving back in Woking at 1:30 am. My jacket reeked, so I took it to the back of the house and draped it on the wrought iron garden bench before I went in.

What a night! I wondered what Henrietta would have said if she'd been in at the time. I lay awake throughout most of the night, replaying the adventure in my head over and over. My stomach churned, and my joints jelled with a dull ache, and I finally fell into a tumultuous sleep.

At *The Toenail* the following day, Pete listened as I recounted my adventure. For the first time, he was the dumbfounded audience, although I couldn't be sure whether his reticence was due to my going off against his good advice. But I enjoyed the fact that, for once, I was James Bond instead of Jamie Blunder. I wasn't just Mickey Mouse, I was Batman and Superman rolled into one invincible super being. I was the Black Panther and not just the black pants.

Nothing happened for the next five days or so. Life returned to normal, and I went back to being plain old me, though I enjoyed the constant memory of that night. I hadn't heard from Eve, and I'd assumed that was the end of it until Pete told me that the police had been to *The Toenail*, asking questions. He didn't tell them anything as he wasn't sure if I'd like to tell the police what I knew or didn't know.

I thought about it for a minute and said, "I'd rather not. Let's wait and see, shall we?"

Looking at me through the top of his ivory-rimmed glasses, he shook his head. "Well, I hate to say I told you so, but I warned you not to go with her that night, didn't I? What will your dear wife say when she gets back and finds the police sniffing around your shady affairs?"

"Doubt it will come to that," I laughed. After all, I'd done nothing wrong.

I got the letter and pictures the next day. As usual I'd lain in until 10:30 am and only found the day's post on the indoor foot mat as I laboured down the creaky stairs. I knew at once that the large brown envelope with no stamp, nestling among the rest of the letters, was no junk mail. My name and address was scrawled in sloping, spidery handwriting with a blue felt-tip pen. At the bottom, it said "DO NOT DESTROY THIS ENVE-LOPE".

I opened it with trembling hands, not due to apprehension, but because my hands always trembled when I was concentrating on any minor task. Fine motor skills, my 32-year-old son Marty had often maintained with unhelpful prescience, were usually the first to go during the irrevocable process of ageing.

A set of 4½-inch photographs fell out of the envelope, and I found myself staring at a clear picture of myself dancing with Eve in that barmy London club. Judging by my smile, it was clear that I was having a whale of a time. There was another picture of me looking down the sumptuous cleavage of a young, buxom reveller. My face looked like the mug shot of an unrepentant pervert.

An involuntary chuckle welled up in my tummy and bubbled through my throat. A middle-aged man having fun - surely there was nothing wrong with that, I thought. But that was before I saw the last photo, which had dropped face down on to the hallway rug. It showed me reclining, with Eve on her knees, head pressed down into my groin, her face obscured by my bare buttocks. My face was turned towards the camera and I had the weirdest expression I'd ever seen.

I dropped the photograph as if it were a searing hot poker, and fled towards the nearest chair, sinking gratefully into it as my heartbeat raced towards a dangerous finishing line. The thing in the photo did not happen, of course. I was sure of that. It had to have been made up. Yet, on no account would I want anyone to see it.

I pulled myself together and gathered the envelope and photos from where I'd dropped them. There was a note. The writing was the same as the one on the envelope but in capital letters.

"YOU MUST PAY £20,000 TO SAVE YOUR ROT-TEN REPUTATION AND YOUR MARRIAGE. PUT CASH IN THIS ENVELOPE. TAKE THE 486 BUS TO GUILDFORD AND DROP THE ENVELOPE IN THE BIN AT THE ELM ST. BUS STOP, AT 7:45 PM TOMOR-ROW EVENING. DO NOT INVOLVE THE POLICE. DO AS WE SAY OR THE PICTURES WILL BE SENT TO YOUR LOVELY WIFE."

I didn't know what to do. This sort of thing only happened on TV or in books. I put the note and pictures back in the envelope and slipped it behind the book-shelf. Then I threw on some decent clothes and set off to *The Dragon's Toenail* to see Pete. He was the only one I knew who'd listen and might have some useful advice.

The pub was shut, which was unusual at the time. I loitered in front of the black oak double doors for a moment and then, not knowing what else to do, I wandered round to the back of the building. One of the windows on the first floor was slightly ajar, and I could hear what sounded like a full-blown argument ema-nating from within. I stiffened to attention when I heard the unmistakable screech that was Eve's voice. Although I could not make out what was being said, I knew at once that Pete was not to be trusted. Of course, he had everything to do with my current predicament. Only then did I remember that I'd told Pete about my redun-dancy compensation, a lump sum of £20,000 - a surplus windfall still languishing in our joint savings account, its fate as yet undecided. He'd asked me to go into partnership in his pub business, and I'd laughed at the time and said "What? And end up buying my own Guinness twice over? Surely that'll ruin the taste."

He'd laughed too, but only with his voice and not his eyes. And that was the end of that conversation.

I wasted no time hanging around *The Toenail*. Going to the police was not a particularly attractive option, since Henrietta would obviously not believe anything I said if any of this came to light - especially with that awful photo. Besides, the incident with Tina, so many years before, would resurface once again; a moment of minor indiscretion blown out of all proportion.

I had to think pretty fast.

Henrietta was due back the following day - the same day I was to drop the blackmail money.

I thought of calling Marty, but suspected he'd only panic and call his mum. So I decided to see what I could find on the internet. I used to spend a lot of time on the laptop that Marty had bought me for my 60th, but I'd later found it all too overwhelming, the way information flew at you from all directions, making unreasonable demands on your time and attention. It was interfering with my sedate way of life, so I'd abandoned it at the time.

As I lifted the Toshiba Satellite 400 out of its dusty bag, I wondered if I should find a private investigator, or just scan the discussion groups for possible ideas. But while I was booting up the laptop and waiting for it to connect to the wireless broadband router, I decided it would be better to start by Googling "Peter Alexander of *The Dragon's Toenail*". I was astonished at what I found. First, by following a link of his membership of the Beers and Pubs Association, I found that he'd inherited the pub from his parents, who had died in a luxury holiday cruise accident in Corsica when Pete was only 25. And then I found that he was on the brink of bankruptcy, with several takeover attempts from the owners of his rival, *The Red Lion*.

So, my favourite pub was on borrowed time.

A search for images and pictures yielded a direct hit which caused my eyes to pop, and made me sit up immediately. Among the array of pictures on the screen, there was one of a younger Pete Nolan in his early to mid-thirties and a woman who was a younger version of Eve - same kangaroo smile, same stone-hard eyes, but with different-coloured hair and a different name.

Without hesitation, I Googled "Silvia Manning". There were many images for that name; the most notable of which was in Georgia University, where a Dr Silvia Manning was particularly active in genetics research. Another Silvia Manning was a psychic in Australia whose credentials included the ability to communicate with aliens. But none of them appeared to be the particular Sylvia Manning I was after. I tried "Eve Manning" without any great hopes, and was, therefore, not too disappointed when nothing useful came up.

By the time I wound down my online investigations it was 6 pm. I'd been riveted to the screen for three solid hours. My stomach howled, and my head felt like a helium rubber balloon at the end of a cotton string. But I no longer felt hopeless about my situation. Now I knew who was pulling my chain, I was resolved to call their bluff. Of course, the best thing all round would be for the matter to be put to rest without any of my family knowing anything about it.

I made myself some pasta bolognese, which was the top end of my cooking skills. The orange juice tasted slightly off, but I gulped it down thirstily, remembering that I'd drunk worse. As I wolfed down my meal, I decided on a plan. The best thing to do was to confront Pete and hope that he'd see sense. But either way, I wouldn't part with any money if I could avoid it.

At 8:30 pm I arrived at *The Toenail* as usual, making every effort to maintain my normal composure. I caught Pete's eye and he pulled me a gorgeous pint of Guinness. I smiled and enquired after his health, and he replied as usual, although there was some stiffness in his movements. I sat at my favourite table, in front of the TV screen to enjoy the cricket. It was a replay of the Investec Ashes, and Shoaib had just taken another wicket in one of the fastest-paced games I'd ever watched.

Each time I glanced at Pete he was looking in my direction with one raised eyebrow, but I remained poker-faced and casually turned back to the cricket.

After an hour, he finally wandered over. "Everything okay, Charlie? You look a bit distracted today."

"I'm fine," I said, "What about you? I was thinking the same about you too."

"Me, I'm fine." Then he cleared his throat. "Heard any more from your tatty lady friend?"

"No," I replied. "Have you?"

Then he turned and stared at me first with a scowl and then a nervous smile. "No."

I sighed, and then said, "Pete, I know what you're up to. You and Sylvia..."

"What?" There was a jitter in his voice. I'd caught him off-guard. And even as he denied it, I was sure that he was unconvinced by his own performance.

"I don't know what you're on about."

"I thought we were mates, Pete. I can't believe you could do this to me."

"Sorry, I still don't know what you're talking about."

"I know all about you and Sylvia or Eve or whatever she calls herself. I don't care what you do with those photos. You are not getting a penny out of me."

"Okay. But you will be making a big mistake there. None of this was my idea. It's Sylvia; she had the photos taken, and she did a fabulous trick with Photoshop and produced those naughty pictures. Pretty good, eh? The wonders of technology these days."

"Yeah," I grunted, clasping my hand around the Nokia Communicator in my coat pocket like a traitor's dagger. "Well, shame on you both, that's what I'll say."

Pete's manner had changed completely. Now that he had nothing more to hide, his lips were curved in a triumphant smile, and his chin jutted jeeringly at me. "Look, the way things stand, I don't think you have any choice at all. You've been a naughty boy. Or shall I say a dirty old man?"

My hands trembled, and I sweated as I stood up to leave. Pete called after me, "You know what to do, old boy."

So at 7:30 pm the following day, I boarded the 486 from the Woking central bus stop and headed for the appointed place in Guildford. I followed the instructions carefully and did not once look back. I stopped at the Elm Street bus stop, loitered around there until 7:45 and then walked casually to the designated litter bin and dropped the envelope, convinced that someone was hiding behind the hedges, waiting to pounce on it as soon as I'd left the scene.

I took the same bus back to Woking on return. At *The Daisy Chain* in front of the station, I bought a bunch of pink roses to take home to welcome Henrietta back that evening. She'd been gone for three weeks - my most adventurous three weeks ever. No more misgivings about having lived a mundane, uneventful life. I'd been conned, inhaled marijuana, drunk some awful stuff, been shot at, blackmailed, and carried out my very own DIY investigation. Perhaps, more exciting than anything else, I hoodwinked my blackmailers and sent them a secret recording of their admission in their own envelope. Since then I'd quietly listen to other people's tales with a knowing smile and a secret assurance that I too had once been the main character in a long and twisted tale of my own - provided, of course, that Pete and Sylvia don't suddenly find a way to get one back on me.

Twins

Brenda recognized James at once, and would have succeeded in shutting the door in his face if he hadn't wedged his foot between the door and the jamb. "What do you want?" she asked her twin brother. Even though she hadn't seen him for seven years, she was instantly repelled by his presence. She turned her head away sharply from his weak smile, made even more disgusting by the pink lipstick on his thin lips and the overdone, multi-shade eyelashes.

"Hi, Sis. Long time no see, eh?"

She crowded him off the threshold, towering squarely in front of the open door as she scowled at James, who peered hopefully past her into the dimly-lit flat that emanated welcoming warmth.

"Just a friendly visit. It's been so long..."

"Look, I don't want to talk to you. I don't want to

see you and I don't want to have anything to do with you. If you've come to say something, please say it and go... and don't call me 'Sis'. I am no sister of yours."

"I came here to tell you about Dad."

The edge went out of her voice. "What about Dad?"

She last saw their father two days earlier, at Waltham Cross Nursing Home, where he'd been for six years. It had been downhill for him since their mum had died in that awful motor accident in the autumn of 1984. It was the end of family life as they knew it. The old man had become profoundly disillusioned, quit his vocation as a district health worker, and descended rapidly into melancholy. Soon ill health claimed what was left of him, and he eventually succumbed to early dementia. By the time he was moved to Waltham, he could barely recognize anyone, not even Brenda, who visited him unfailingly every Tuesday.

James never went to see him.

Considering their dad's unconcealed disappointment over James' wimpiness and her own masculinity, Brenda often wondered whether, after all, she was the 'son' he'd never had, and James the 'daughter' he'd never wanted.

What the hell could James have to say about Dad? If the old bugger has finally croaked, the people at the nursing home would have contacted me first.

She stepped aside and let James in, watching him closely. He hadn't changed much despite the years, even though he'd bleached his hair and wore it shoulder length. He wore a tight-fitting blue T-shirt and even tighter black jeans. She was sure he'd had his operation by now.

And it seemed he'd developed an infuriating case of roving eyes syndrome, because, from the moment he entered the flat, his eyes never stopped darting all over the place. Even after he'd sat down on the double sofa in front of the pokey old Philips TV, his beady eyes continued their erratic excursion.

"So, what's it with Dad?" Brenda asked, with no emotion in her voice.

"I was at his bedside earlier today."

Those stupid eyes! Why can't they keep still? I bet he's on some kind of drug... And that goofy grin! If he keeps wrinkling his nose like that, I swear I'll kill him.

"Well, what?"

"I've got no place to stay tonight."

"I don't see how that's my business. Why don't you just go back to Bristol? You can't stay here, that's for sure... And don't give me that stupid look..."

She remembered how she'd always looked out for him in school when the older boys picked on him. It was an awful time for both of them. All the girls in her class had shunned her because she was tall and had enormous hands. It didn't help when, at the age of thirteen, her voice broke and she had to quit the school choir.

"It's too late to get a train to Bristol at this time," he mumbled.

"Then find yourself a B&B, for goodness sake."

"I'm skint, Sis. I don't even have the bus fare to King's Cross."

"You should have bloody thought of that before coming here!" She checked herself as she realized she was starting to raise her voice. Then she tried to scare him off with one final bluff.

"If you don't leave here at once I'll call the police."

"Dad talked."

"What?"

Their dad hadn't spoken a word for the past six years. When she visited, he just stared at her. He only made unintelligible noises, obviously from pain or discomfort, or at other times he would emit a prolonged groan profoundly bereft of purpose or meaning. Brenda did all the talking; telling him about what she was up to in her work as a bouncer at the *Happy Pirates Club* on Hoe Street, most of which he'd surely not have approved of.

"Yes, he talked to me about things."

"Liar. The man is practically brain dead."

"I'm telling you, he did. One of the attendants was there; the short one with ginger eyebrows. She called the other two attendants. You should have seen how excited they were."

Brenda was silent for a moment. *The old bastard. Keeping schtum all these years. Now James pays him one measly visit, and he starts blabbing his head off.*

"So what did he have to say?"

"Will you let me stay or what?"

She did not reply. Instead, she went into the bedroom and shut the door.

James took the opportunity to have a proper look

around. Somewhere in this grubby little flat, he'd find what he was looking for.

The place was like the abode of a Lithuanian monk - tatty but tidy. On the wall was a black and white photo of a man on a vintage motorcycle with exceptionally long telescopic forks.

Which one does she fancy, the man or the bike?

In one corner, there was a classic telephone with a rotary dial, but without a connecting cable. Parked neatly by the bathroom door was a gigantic pair of ballet shoes.

James wandered into the kitchen.

If she catches me snooping around, I'll tell her I'm making myself a cup of tea.

A few plates were stacked on the otherwise bare worktop, and some glass cups, mugs and other cheap utensils were in the overhead cabinet.

Spick and span, our Brenda is. Clean as a weasel. Only trouble is, she's never sure what she wants to be.

There were some cracked tiles on the floor, and dark stains of rising damp on the back wall.

Really done well for yourself, haven't you, Sis?

Far better than he'd done. His girly looks always got in the way of any job prospects. But all that was about to change. Their dad, in one final bout of guilt and regret, had told him about the money Uncle Fred had bequeathed to him and Brenda. From a very early age, Uncle Fred had always tried to teach them to be wise with money. He'd set up a joint savings account for them and given them the pass-book as a present on their tenth birthday. There was only £10 in the kitty to start with, and, although they had never saved any more money despite Uncle Fred's constant advice, Brenda had always kept the pass-book. Knowing Brenda, James was sure that somewhere in the flat there would be a box containing some old photos from their primary school days, several dolls in varying stages of damage or dismemberment, some of their mum's jewellery, and the pass-book.

Unknown to Brenda, the pass-book was now worth 60 grand. Uncle Fred had been putting some money in the savings account all along, and he'd deposited a substantial lump sum shortly before he died. Only their father knew about it, but he didn't think they deserved the money and so hadn't felt compelled to mention it.

If James could get his hands on that pass-book, he would forge his sister's signature, and all that money would be his. She didn't even have to know about it. She was doing okay, anyway. If she knew, she would cheat him of his rightful share. *The selfish, overbearing bitch.*

Brenda remained in her self-imposed incarceration for over an hour. By then James had satisfied himself that the pass-book could only be in the bedroom. He'd quaffed three cups of tea and was curled up on the sofa like a Munchkin cat, using his rucksack as a headrest, and watching the Jerry Springer late night show.

She'd changed into her work clothes - a black sleeveless top and a pair of black combat trousers. Her effort to powder over her red-rimmed eyes and her determination to keep her expression hard and unfriendly did nothing to hide her troubled state of mind.

"OK, you can stay, but only for tonight." Her Adam's apple juddered as she swallowed. "I don't care for your silly games over Dad's condition. I want your sorry arse out of my flat first thing tomorrow."

"I don't want to push my luck, Sis, but is there any chance of something to eat?"

No reply.

James was dismayed to see that she was holding a key.

The bitch, she's locked the bloody bedroom door.

She stared at him and waggled her Adam's apple as if she was about to say something, then she turned around to leave.

"When are you coming back?"

"I'm working through the night; I'll be back around seven." She hesitated.

What am I doing, leaving all my belongings in the hands of this - stranger?

But she left without saying another word.

"Ciao!" James chimed gleefully.

He pottered about the flat for a while.

If I damn well have to break down that door, I will. And once I get that pass-book, I'm gone.

But when he turned the handle, he was surprised to see that the door was not locked after all. He stepped gingerly into the mixed aroma of sandalwood powder and cheap perfume. The bed dominated most of the space, with a small dressing table on one side. The embroidery on the pillow reminded him of the needlework he'd done when he was 13. When he picked up the pillow, he found an old leather-bound book underneath it.

What do we have here?... Brenda's diary! He picked it up at once. *What? An entry for every single day! Sis must have too much time.*

Her handwriting was neat, but the words leaned forward as if they were standing in the middle of a Mediterranean gale. Most of the pages were stained, and some of the words were smudged.

\#

...Today, I was sitting all by myself in Lloyd Park, watching the people milling around. If only I were part of the crowd. I'm fed up with being an outsider all the time...

\#

James chuckled. *Awww... poor Sis, how my heart bleeds for you!*

\#

... Visited Dad at the nursing home today. I don't think he will ever get better. I tried to cheer him up with the joke about the randy monk, but he just stared at me with those dead eyes. I miss the old Dad, even though he was never there. I also miss Mum and J...

...

... Stayed in all day today. I didn't even bother to switch on the light when it was getting dark. I wonder what J is up to? Why do I feel so lost? It felt like half of me was ripped apart when we both went our separate ways – like it was only yesterday. I feel incomplete...

...

... Today I won £10 in the lottery. If I won a million, I would give it all away just to make up with J.

#

But the entry that was to cause James the worst heartache was yet to come.

#

... I will never forgive J for telling Mum and Daddy about Jeanette and me, but I would give my right arm to see him again. Why did he have to go so far away and never get in touch? I will not be the first to make contact, that's for sure.

#

But Bristol was dad's idea. He said it was all for the best. When I called, he said you didn't want anything to do with me, the devious old bastard!

By the time Brenda returned, James had read through the whole diary twice. He'd completely forgotten about the pass-book. He was sitting on the bed, just as he'd been four hours earlier, staring at the open diary and trembling, his eyes streaming with tears, his Adam's apple hurting like hell.

Weight of Friendship

Everything about Lucy was wrong. There wasn't a single redeeming feature. Her head was oddly-shaped; similar in every respect to a Mongolian pumpkin. From under her pile of thick black Jeri curls loomed a face that lacked symmetry, elegance and grace. Her eyes were spaced slightly too far apart, the left one just a little off-level, giving her the appearance of a discontented shark. Lucy was the only person capable of focusing her gaze on two things at the same time. Her eyes roved in-dependently, each one on a separate errand.

Just one look at Lucy and I quickly turned away. I'd seen many ugly faces in my time, but Lucy's took pole spot in my mental gallery of horror masks. I stole another look. No, it wasn't a hallucination. There she was; a head the size of a military tank, ears like a couple of over-done samosas, and a humongous nose that would cause a pelican to gape with envy or heave with disgust, depending on its mood at the time. And those eyes! They were like a pair of roving searchlights manned by a couple of deranged technicians. Now I couldn't look away because one of them was aimed at me on full beam, and the other was casually inspecting the "No Smoking" sign beneath the ventilation hatch.

She must have noticed my trepidation because her thick lips curled back in what could only be a malicious sneer, unveiling a row of jagged, discoloured teeth.

I switched on what was intended to be a charming smile, but I don't think I totally pulled it off. From the tautness of my face muscles I knew this smile was no more than a doleful grimace - the sort you'd expect to find on the face of a chemistry professor drowning in a sea of synthetic goose fat.

I fully expected her to yell at me, "What the hell are you gawking at, you twerp?" To which I would reply... Well, no, I wouldn't have replied, actually, because this human aberration, this grotesque apparition, left me totally speechless.

The second eye finally joined its colleague, and now both of them bored into me like a dentist's drill. The thought occurred to me that each eye had a personality of its own, and they could well have been two aberrant quacks evaluating my mental health and for once coming to a unanimous consensus that I was woefully unstable. Or they could be two cops, one bad and one nasty, interrogating me before torture. We were locked in a staring match. I was clearly outnumbered and certainly didn't stand a chance.

Then slowly, a terrifying realization dawned on me, the way disaster casts a lengthening shadow of doom on a village about to be consumed by a tsunami. There was a chance - just a chance - that she was smiling. It just could be that a real smile was beyond the capability of that unearthly face and that what I had there before me was the best she could do. So, determined to return her bizarre manifestation of politeness, I once again tried to rearrange my face muscles into the semblance of a smile, and say "Hello". But the word came out like a half squeak, half giggle, like the utterance of a piglet in distress. I just couldn't stop. It was like trying to suppress an insistent fart that had been insisting for far too long. You know the sort of flatulence which no amount of bottom clenching can prevent from escaping, the type my dad calls the "Houdini fart"? It comes out louder than it would have done if you simply let it go without a struggle. The only difference this time was that it was like farting from the mouth. I just couldn't help myself. My throat burnt up, and my eyes watered as I strained to suppress a bout of hysterical laughter.

By now there was no doubt that other people in the train were looking at me. A middle-aged accountant in a mottled grey suit and a howling, bright, floral silk tie was staring. He had the expression of an inquisitive ostrich. I couldn't tell whether he was angry or just sorry for me. A thin young redhead in a brown pleated jumper stared contemptuously as she blew up her bubble gum until the flimsy balloon popped and spread out over her lower chin. I looked at her long arms and short legs and wondered if she'd borrowed them from a teenage chimp. She continued looking severely in my direction for a while before turning away in disgust. Everybody else was either staring at the ceiling or at the floor.

Then I had a fantastic idea.

I could always count on my wits to quickly come to my rescue in times of embarrassment, which were not few and far between. I remembered when I'd referred to Mandy Longbottom, my course manager at St Mary's in Cambridge, as "comprising entirely of breasts", only to find she was standing right behind me. So I'd immediately added "... And not just any old breasts, of course." I thought I had pulled it off, but she never spoke to me again. There was another time when I joked about Terry's gout and then quickly converted it into a witty compliment when I noticed the disgust on everyone's face.

Putting my new idea into action, I broke out into a convulsive sneeze, which was designed to disguise the offensive giggles. In an instant, I converted my embarrassment into a helplessness that demanded real sympathy. I sent out a clear and unequivocal message that my windpipe had gone into an independent anaphylactic convulsion, and I was about to die. It was an overwhelming success. I was so pleased with the result that I made a mental note to patent this ingenious new crisis management strategy. I'd call it the "Aristocratic Sneagle".

Lucy's expression hadn't changed - or maybe there wasn't any way of knowing. She still stared at me with that weird look.

I spluttered on, glad to be doing something to minimize the ridiculous tension that would have been brought on by my odd behaviour. I began to wonder whether I was just making a bigger ass of myself than I needed to. But at that point it actually didn't matter.

And then she spoke.

Her voice sounded like wet gravel falling on toughened glass. It had the timbre of an off-key trombonist and the pitch of an altar boy caught by surprise at the precise instance that his voice had just broken.

"Are you alright, dear?" she gargled.

Compounding the shock was her East End accent, which brought to mind an inept impressionist doing Margaret Thatcher's voice, talking with a nose full of premium quality Ambrosia custard.

Her entire demeanour just didn't agree with what she'd said. She could more easily have said, "Would you like me to pull out your tongue and wrap it round your head five times, and then tie it in a double constrictor knot?" to which I'd quite naturally have replied, "Err... No." Or she could have said, "Now, what if I rip out your left eye and nail it to a yellow lamp post?" And I still wouldn't have said, "Yes, thanks ma'am."

"Are you okay?"

I raised one hand to my face and then, waving the other hand helplessly, I brought my 'sneagle' performance to a grand finale with a flourish - a final splutter which gracefully diminished into a series of smaller coughs.

She got up from her seat. As she sailed towards me, I burst into a fresh fit of 'sneagles'. I couldn't help it because she looked even more ridiculous full height and at close quarters. I simply didn't know where to look, what to say or what to think. I'd certainly never seen anyone like her before. You couldn't say she was enormous; that would have belittled her obesity. No word had yet been invented for her, and even if one were, it would still require decoration.

By some sheer miracle, she'd stuffed herself into a green blouse and a pair of tarpaulin jeans. The blouse strained at the seams until it seemed it was ready to burst. The front buttons held on for dear life, the top button having popped off (I imagined that it would have been catapulted for thousands of miles at the time of the incident, hitting a baby elephant between the eyes somewhere in central Africa and knocking it stone dead). Lucy's cleavage was dark and deep, and as menacing as a crocodile-infested waterhole. Presently it seemed her breasts were competing with each other to see which one would win the "bursting melon" competition. Everything - even bits that weren't supposed to move - wobbled.

Finally, she dumped herself on to the entire bank of three seats opposite mine. She leaned across and placed one fat hand on my shoulder. I might as well have been lugging an oversized clump of tropical bananas.

"All right, luv?" she grated once again.

I had no choice now. I had to put my sneezing and giggling on hold. I had to get a grip. With such a heavy weight on my shoulder, I had absolutely no choice.

"I'm sorry," I spluttered. "I've got an awfully tickly throat."

Perhaps she should have asked why my awful throat only began to tickle after I'd set eyes on her scary face. Instead, she said she'd only just recovered from a nasty cold herself. She thought there might be a bug on the loose.

"By the way," she said, taking the bananas off my shoulders, "my name is Lucy. I'm going to be a model."

A model? Now, that certainly got me. My stomach knotted into a quivering and excruciating ball of un-controllable delirium. *A model of what?* A weird, wild, laughter spurted out of my mouth like projectile vomit.

She loaded the bananas back on my shoulders, and I immediately calmed down.

"I'm Henry," I heard myself saying. A sinking apprehension gripped me immediately, and I almost panicked. What if she offered a handshake? How would I know which banana to grab?

She uttered a brief, unearthly sound that I only hoped was meant to be a friendly chuckle.

After that, she launched into a mesmerizing mono-logue, lasting over fifteen minutes.

She was a part-time student doing her third year of a diploma in media studies at City University. She'd lived in Birmingham with her parents until she decided to go out into the world and set herself on the path towards a massive career. She was going to be BIG! (Any bigger, dear, I thought, and the whole universe will be filled with the mess of your explosion). She worked part-time as a waitress, and she was into modelling. She'd done a couple of photo-shoots, and she might soon bag an exclusive contract offer. "Watch this space," she'd said. I sighed, wondering if she hadn't taken all the space already. She lived in a small flat in Deptford and had a cat named Lobster. She didn't seem to want to know anything about me. It appeared that all she wanted of me was to shut up and listen. Intimidated by the bananas, I genuinely had no choice.

She was going to get off the train at Woolwich Arsenal. As we approached the station she said, "It's been very nice meeting you," and then she smiled (yes, by this time I knew that expression was a smile). She pushed her address book in front of me and said, "Should keep in touch, yeah?"

I wrote down "Henry" and added my mobile number.

She wrote something on a piece of paper, leant over and put it in my top pocket. Then she ambled out of the train. She turned round and waved a clump of bananas at me, and I watched her as she wobbled away.

The only thing I remembered about the rest of the night was a vague surprise that I'd been so smashed after only a few pints of Staropramen I'd had with Matt before I went on that train. I hadn't counted, but it couldn't have been more than three pints. The only way I could have been that wasted was if that scoundrel had slipped something into my beer. I couldn't even tell how I'd made it to the flat.

I didn't mention my encounter with Lucy to Tim, my flatmate and best friend, until after a week or so. Too embarrassed over how drunk I had been that day, I simply wanted to forget the whole incident. But he found the piece of paper in my pocket as he was sorting out our laundry.

I watched as a scowl crawled across his rat-like face. He carefully unfolded the paper and peered at it in a way only he could peer at things, apart from the *Myotis alcathoe*, of course - that rare species of vermin that squinted in the dark.

"Maggot!"

That was his nickname for me. Our friendship followed the maxim that much contempt resulted from excessive familiarity. As ours was the most familiar of friendships, it therefore transpired that the true measure of our camaraderie was the quality of contempt we lavished on each other.

"Ha. The rodent squeaks."

"What is this?" he accused. "You aren't going to the *Showcase Cinema* to watch *Avatar* all by your own maggoty self, are you?"

The trouble with Tim was that he was in the habit of constantly leaping headlong into the wrong conclusions the way a lemming seeks the edge of a cliff. But I soon realized it was the paper Lucy had put in my pocket. I'd forgotten about it completely.

"It's not mine, Rodent. Someone put it in my pocket. A girl I met."

"The maggot met a girl! Ha ha ha..." his haughty snigger bounced around the walls of the dingy flat like the beam of a torchlight in the hands of a juvenile prankster. "You're kidding, right?"

"No. I met her on the train."

"So, after all these years, you finally pulled, eh?"

I smiled. Wait until you see the thing that I pulled, I thought. But suddenly, realizing that Tim had become rather envious, I desisted from divulging my first impressions of Lucy.

The trouble with Tim was, despite his appearance and legendary lack of success getting a date, he was a ladies' man at heart. He'd avidly devoured two entire leather-bound volumes of *The Ancient Art of Medieval Wench-Dating* by Edgar J Edgar, which had been out of print since 1917. He was constantly debating the merits of the "shock and awe" technique over the "catchy monkey" approach, neither of which I suspected could be legal ways of going about getting a girl's attention in modern civilization. Tim was always boasting about his knowledge of the ancient Egyptian secret of *Armunapon*, which was guaranteed to make you utterly irresistible in the eyes of any female - human or beast. Often he'd set out to put it into practice, only for his courage to desert him at the very last minute. There was something about his personality that always caused girls to walk the other way when they spotted him from a distance. It was as if all female species had been equipped with a sure-fire early warning system specifically to alert them against a possible encounter with Tim Daluma.

Well, it's not often that a girl slips a cinema ticket in your pocket while you are on the train, drugged to your eyeballs with some unknown substance. Now I was enjoying the envy that dripped from poor Tim's voice.

"So, why haven't you called her then, this metro babe of yours?"

"She's not my type."

"Uh, Maggot, since when did you start developing such high tastes in women?"

"Anyway, I don't have her phone number."

"But that's what she's written at the back of this ticket, you worm."

So it was.

But what if she didn't know that she'd written her number on a valuable bit of paper? She might be missing the ticket. I realized that I would have to call her, especially as Tim was staring at me with his ratty eyes, obviously expecting me to do something courageous.

It took some guts to make that call. It wasn't before I'd climbed the seven hills of *Ahuja* - a set of ridiculous ritual drills which I'd invented and often used to psych myself up before facing the most extreme challenges. These included a *Mazumba* war dance and a deep-throated Maori chant. I tapped the keyboard of my phone as if it were made of eggshell and braced myself as it began to ring.

The voice that replied at the other end of the line

was not anything like what I'd heard on the train, but I knew at once it was her. And then I suddenly realized I hadn't rehearsed what I was going to say.

"Y-you left your cinema ticket..." I stuttered.

"Of course, I know. I bought two. I've still got the other ticket. Where should we meet before the film?"

"I didn't - "

"Greenhithe Station at 7:30 pm. We'll take the bus to Bluewater."

I performed a desperate mental Google for a suitable excuse but drew a blank. The widening gulf of silence was becoming embarrassing.

"OK," I yielded.

"It's a date," she chimed, and the line went dead.

"A date!" Tim echoed with excitement. He'd heard every single word. He beamed at me, oblivious of my dismay.

I soon found myself pacing up and down the tiny room.

"Maggot, will you please stop fidgeting - it's a date, not a public execution."

I paced the length of the room one more time, then turned around.

"Timbo, why don't you go in my place? This girl, she's more your type. You always said you like a big backside. You wait until you see her. She's got backsides coming out of her ears."

A lustful glint flashed in Tim's ratty eyes.

"Don't you think she'd be annoyed if someone else turned up instead of you?"

"No, Tim. She'll fall for you as soon as she sets eyes on you. Trust me, I know."

Tim beamed.

He'd leap at any opportunity for a date. Even if it was with Mother Teresa come back from the sacred grave without make-up. This was a ready-made opportunity. Tim only had to turn up at the station, apologize on his friend's behalf and let his irresistible charm do the rest.

Before I met Tim, I'd never had any real mates. It was while I was a student at Cambridge - my alma mater from which I'd dropped out after my first year. We'd met at a conference arranged by UNESCO for socially challenged, low-achieving African students. I attended the conference only out of curiosity, although it had initially been brought to my notice by my course director, who was convinced it was an opportunity to improve on my already excellent social skills. Excellent in spite of certain, minor, seemingly unsociable traits that normally caused most decent people to look away. Her reasoning was that I would be "in my element" among misfits of the same ilk.

I remember wandering around in the hall during the buffet lunch, trying to deploy my aforementioned networking skills, but not finding anybody suitably vulnerable to inflict them upon. There must have been eighty people or so, standing in groups of twos and threes, making vaguely intellectual noises of the kind to be heard in conference halls. Feeling like an Indian rhinoceros in a Chinese restaurant, I was starting to wonder what the hell I was doing there when Tim appeared.

"Hi there," he said. "You must be the other delegate from the BSA."

"What?"

"Banania Student Association," he explained.

"I'm not from Banania," I said quickly. "Actually, I'm from Kenya, although I lived in South Africa for most of my early childhood, and attended secondary school in Zimbabwe."

"Sorry, I got you all mixed up. I guess I was just too eager to find a fellow Bananian. Funny thing, it's the other way round with me. People often mistake me for a Kenyan." He laughed.

I laughed too, and then stopped immediately, because I suddenly realized he hadn't actually said anything funny.

He was tall and slim, and his suit hung loosely around him so that he looked like a human coat hanger. He had a slightly raised upper lip that clearly indicated he couldn't possibly be clever. He also had an endearing demeanour of an uncertain quality that marked him out as an authentic specimen of the non-achiever archetype.

He invited me to join the rest of the students in his group. It was the only group with more than three people. They were in the middle of a full-blown discussion about the situation in Africa, and they all had loud voices. It was like a free-for-all cockfight. A tall, charcoal-black guy called James was the loudest. He declared confidently that poverty was invented in America, packaged in the UK and sold, at a substantial premium, to Africans. And even though they were short-changed in the transaction, it had since become their undeniable heritage, which they wore like a cloak of honour.

"No," countered chubby Benson, who had the stature and face of an implacable warthog, "I think you will find that is democracy."

"Demo - what?" Alice was an imposing figure. Everybody listened when she spoke. Her fuzzy hair was made up in a huge bun with a parting in the centre, which made it look as if she had an enormous black arse on her head. She also had enormous breasts, so that in silhouette you would think she was driving a convertible Volkswagen Beetle - or wearing one.

"The Republic of Banania is the headquarters of corruption," she declared, "thanks to ex-President Vincent Adamu and his government, who placed the country on the map of infamy through their outstanding corrupt practices."

"Adamu was a bloody pig!" shouted James, triggering a raucous clamour of approval from the rest.

But Tim had a different view. "Come on, guys. Let's not get bogged down with bitterness and negativity." In a flash, he'd suddenly acquired the air of a politician-in-waiting, speaking slowly and deliberately. "We need to think about how to make things better. We need to put aside the failings of the past and present governments, and think of a way forward out of this mess."

"Bravo!" It was James again, clapping in mock ovation. "Considering how your dad was treated by Adamu and his government for defending the peoples' rights... Every time the poor guy opened his mouth he was thrown into jail. And the prisons in Banania make London's Belmarsh look like the *Hotel La Perouse* in Paris."

I didn't have anything to contribute to the discussion. The ignorance of people like James and Alice was a minor irritation I'd learnt to live with over the years. It was like being stuck in a lift freshly fouled by a flatulent fool - all you could do was stand there and endure it. What did they know about politics? What did they know about being in charge of millions of people, most of whom were lazy, good-for-nothing illiterates? What would they have done with a worthless troublemaker like Dr Daluma, whose mission in life was to make governing impossible by trying to enlighten the public about things they were better off not knowing about? Why didn't he accept the lucrative government appointment that was offered to him, and keep his ugly mouth shut?

I wasn't ashamed of my father, but for my own self-preservation and the chance of ever making any friends, I had to lie about who I was. I had to resort to my mother's maiden name, Raponsawe. It was my good luck that my father had been President of the Republic of Banania for more than fourteen years, during which I was cosseted, pampered and thoroughly spoilt in a luxurious environment. But it wasn't my fault things didn't go so well during my father's time in office.

That conference was more than five years ago. I dropped out of Cambridge, but Timothy completed his degree at the University of Portsmouth with a 2.2 in economics. We'd been best friends, and gatecrashed many dodgy parties together. He continued to believe I was a farmer's son from Kenya, who had bungled his scholarship to the University of Surrey. As far as he knew, I was too ashamed to return to my country, and I never wanted to discuss the matter ever again.

It was past 11 pm, and I expected Tim to be back from his date with Lucy. I had watched everything there was to be watched on our little TV, which could be switched on and off only with a pair of pliers. Tim had cooked some spaghetti bolognese, which I only needed to heat up in the microwave when the need arose. The need had arisen more than thrice, and all the pasta was gone. By midnight, I could no longer contain my anxiety, so I called Tim's mobile. It went straight to voice mail. I didn't think it wise or proper to call Lucy at that time. Especially not after I'd failed to go with her, but had sent my imbecile friend instead. Perhaps no news was good news after all. I reluctantly went to bed, assuring myself that Tim was a grown-up and could therefore look after himself.

Tim didn't return until 10 am the next day, something that had never happened since I'd known him. I hadn't had breakfast by then, mainly because Tim usually made breakfast. I couldn't help noticing that he looked bedraggled. His oversized suit jacket had curled up around the lapels, and there were grime stains on his shirt sleeves. The seat of his trousers was also smeared. Tim could have easily passed for a hobo who'd slummed the night out on the street, but his grumpiness dissuaded me from any form of sarcasm.

"The rodent returns!" I saluted cautiously.

It seemed the most appropriate insult because at no other time had I known him to look more like a shrew. But to my growing unease, no insult was returned. Not a word was uttered. Clearly, he was deeply upset about something. He wouldn't respond to anything I said afterwards. When I asked what had gone wrong with the date, he turned away and stomped off to the bedroom. I could only conclude that the date had not been a roaring success.

I'd long stopped insulting him and, presently, resorted to begging him. But it didn't change his mood one iota. Within twenty minutes, he'd packed his meagre possessions into his battered suitcase. He tossed his key on the coffee table and slammed the door behind him as he left. I immediately realized that I was in serious trouble, as I'd come to depend on Tim so much. I wasn't going to last five minutes without him.

I called Lucy's mobile. I had no right, of course, and I'd deserve it if she rained insults on me from the other end. She might not even bother to pick up the phone. After all, I hadn't been a gentleman. I squeezed my eyes shut as I waited. But I was surprised by the calm, even pleasant, voice that came through.

"Hey, Henry, is that you? You missed a terrific film... Would've enjoyed it better if I'd had the pleasure of your company."

Then she laughed, and it wasn't anything like the alien racket I'd heard on the train. "Are you OK, though?" she asked.

"Sorry about not being able to come. I sent my friend Tim... Did you meet him?"

There was a brief silence at the other end.

I waited, wondering if she had been offended about me sending Tim, and was about to tell me off in the strongest terms. But instead, she just said, "Hey, why don't we meet up? What are you up to at the moment?"

We arranged to meet at the Burger King in Woolwich at 2 pm. I was there ten minutes early, and after waiting for about twenty minutes, I began to wonder whether Lucy was about to exact her revenge by not turning up.

I'd just finished my second lemonade when she breezed in.

"Henry!"

I almost fell off the cheap Burger King plastic chair.

Surely this wasn't the same person I had seen on the train? She wasn't slender by any account, but certainly not as gross as the aberration that had been brought on by the stuff that rascal, Matt, had poisoned my brain with. I swore right then that I'd never take any alcohol again.

She had on a woolly green top and a pair of blue jeans, and her shoulder-length Jerry curls framed a pleasant and cheerful face with a pair of sparkling eyes. She wasn't bad looking at all.

She didn't sit down until I stood up, pecked her proffered left cheek and then pulled back her chair for her to sit.

"Erm... I'm sorry about..." I began to recite the apology I'd prepared and practised earlier to absolute perfection.

But she shook her head and waved her hands. "It's OK, don't worry about it."

"Let me get you a drink," I offered.

"Nothing for me, please," she said. "I'm on a diet."

I looked on as she proceeded to fill me in on the film in a long and excruciating monologue that ran like an express train that couldn't possibly be stopped. I couldn't understand why this strange, talkative woman would pick me out in a train and invite me on a date to watch a film, especially in the state I was in at the time.

"No, no, I don't want to give it away - I'm sure you might want to watch it at some point..." she was saying. But that didn't stop her narrating the entire plot of the film.

Although it was now clear that she hadn't met Tim, I decided to ask her all the same.

"No, I didn't meet your friend. I called your number several times afterwards, but it just went straight through to your voice mail."

"I'm so sorry," I repeated. "I'm an idiot and a fool."

"No. No. No..."

And then a little later, she asked, "So, what's this

about your friend?"

I told her about Tim Daluma, about our long friendship and how he'd packed his possessions and left without a word.

"I don't have any idea where he's gone, and he's not even answering his mobile," I lamented.

"It's not good for friends to break up. Give me his mobile number. Let me talk to him."

I wasn't sure what she was going to say to him, but I was at least relieved that she'd listened with patience and sympathy. By 7 pm, when we finally left Burger King, it felt as if I had known her for years.

I didn't feel like going straight back to the empty flat, so after I'd seen Lucy off at the train station, I wandered through Woolwich market, which was still quite busy, even though it was dark. I bought a doner kebab at Sidiq's shop and devoured it on the way to the flat.

The ringing of my mobile catapulted me out of bed around 8:30 the next morning.

"Hello, is that you, Tim?" I asked.

I'd called his number several more times after I'd spoken to Lucy, and he'd picked up and promptly cut off the line each time.

"Hi, Henry!"

It turned out to be Lucy. I did my best to sound cheerful. "Hi, Lucy. What a pleasure to hear your angelic voice."

She laughed, and then proceeded to tell me about

her voice-coaching lesson. She planned to start a band soon and was going on *The X Factor*. Without warning, she burst out into a rendition of Whitney Houston's *I Will Always Love You*.

"That will be four yeses," I declared in my best impression of Simon Cowell.

She laughed again, and I thought she was really sweet. She reminded me of Rosemary, my primary school crush. In the past, I hadn't given much time or thought to girls. I'd been too busy worrying over my exile status and had deferred all such matters until I finally returned to Banania. But now, with Lucy, I was starting to get those strange feelings.

"I spoke to Tim," she said.

That brought me back to full attention. "What - what did he say?"

"He's very upset with you because you've fed him too many porkies."

"Porkies?"

"Yes, Henry. Lies. Big, fat lies."

I immediately knew what it was.

"He met this bloke called James on his way to the station. The guy spilled the beans, Henry. Tim knows who you are."

I had nothing to say. I felt a dull ache in my chest, and my throat went dry.

"Henry... Are you still there?" Lucy called.

"I'm sorry," I finally said, fully convinced that she and Tim would have nothing to do with me any more.

"Look, I'm meeting up with Tim at the library later

on. I guess I can talk some sense into him. Let's face it, whatever your dad did, it wasn't your fault."

"Thanks Lucy, very kind of you..."

"No worries."

"Perhaps I should come along..."

"No! He doesn't want to see you just yet. But I'm sure it'll soon be sorted. I'll call you back later. Maybe we can meet up at Pizza Hut for a quick bite."

"Thanks Lucy, you're a star."

"I know," she said. And the line went dead.

I spent the rest of the day waiting for Lucy's call. I guessed she had as much chance of persuading Jerry to become Tom's number one fan. But at least I knew she would pass on my apology, for all it was worth.

A plaintive gurgle from the depths of my stomach reminded me that lunch was well overdue. How I missed Tim already. I discovered a cache of Mars bars in the top cupboard above the small fridge. I quickly tucked in, grateful for the reassuring fact that chocolate bars were immune from expiry.

It was 6 pm and I still hadn't heard from Lucy. Obviously she hadn't managed to convince Tim and wasn't going to call just to say that. But I wanted to know what was happening, so I called her mobile. No reply. After a few more attempts, I finally gave up.

The Crazy Frog tune from my mobile jolted me out of my slumber at 9 pm. I was instantly fully conscious. Must be the divine Lucy, I thought, calling to give me the bad news. But the voice that sounded from the phone wasn't Lucy's.

"Maggot by name, maggot by nature, eh?"

"Tim!"

He was on his way to the flat. In the meantime, I called Lucy once again to find out how she'd done it, but all I got was her voice mail. It was such a relief to have Tim back.

"Son of a maggot!" he crowed, his rat face even rattier than ever, albeit with a hint of suspicion and caution in his eyes. He parked his battered suitcase by the bedroom door.

"Is that you, Rodent?"

"It was a shock to find out I'd been living with the son of my father's enemy all these years, the son of President Adamu, who sent my father to jail so many times."

"Sorry, Tim," was all I could say.

Tim was full of admiration for Lucy. "What a lovely girl. I've never met anyone quite like her."

"Yes," I agreed. "She's one in a million. But what did she say to make you change your mind?"

"Nothing really, she just said none of this was your fault... Yada, yada, yada... You know. She talked about friendship, loyalty and forgiveness - all that stuff. A real sweet girl she is."

And then he said, "I think I've finally found my soul mate." At which point my heart sank into my socks. *"She's my soul mate!"* my mind screamed, *"Not yours!"* But I put a lid on my thoughts and heartily welcomed my best friend back to the flat.

Neither of us heard from Lucy that night. I called

again in the morning, but, once again, it went straight through to her voice mail. The whole day passed, and I still didn't hear from her. Tim was showing similar signs of restlessness. He said that after he'd seen her the previous day, she was going for her voice-coaching lesson before heading back home. But neither of us knew exactly where she lived. It irritated me slightly, though, to observe the tenderness with which Tim spoke of her.

As another day passed without any word from Lucy, I became more concerned. I wanted to tell her I was so grateful to her for restoring my friendship with Tim, and maybe I wanted to tell her a lot more. Tim was also trying to make contact with Lucy, but although he was more proactive than me, going back to the library where they had last met and making enquiries, he didn't appear to have achieved much success. He even put a soppy ad in *News Shopper* - the Woolwich and Lewisham local newspaper.

On the fifth day, at the absolute limits of despair, I made another call to her mobile, not really expecting anything. I was surprised to get a reply.

"Hello." It was gruff and weary, clearly a man's voice, unless Lucy's voice-coaching had gone spectacularly awry. But at least I was relieved to get a response from her phone.

"Lucy..?"

The voice was flat, mirthless and bored. "Lucy is in hospital."

A thousand thoughts flashed through my mind at

once.

"She's been hospitalized since Thursday. She was run over by a motorbike."

The voice belonged to her Somalian immo flatmate who had come to be the custodian of her mobile phone and her cat.

"She's in St Mary's Hospital."

Tim had been out all day. I called his phone several times but just wasn't getting through. I swore at him for always buying cheap mobiles on crappy Vodafone contracts. I'd hoped we could both visit Lucy in the hospital.

I slapped on my favourite fake leather jacket, crammed my feet into my boots and vaulted out of the flat like a vampire out of purgatory, flagging down the first taxi that came into sight. I was outside St Mary's in thirty minutes flat. I spotted a flower stall by the entrance and picked up a modest bouquet of pink carnations and yellow chrysanthemums. My heart thumped in my chest like no heart had ever thumped before. Jimi Hendrix and Rory Gallagher had teamed up in a once-in-a-lifetime monster rave, and they were hammering out an infernal rock jam session in my left ventricle, the remaining three chambers duly occupied by stomping revellers. My stomach churned, my legs wobbled and my head hurt with intense apprehension and overwhelming anxiety. I knew then that I was in love, and I swore at myself for the way the dodgy beer had warped my senses the first time I'd met Lucy on that train, and caused me to see an aberration - a

Mongolian pumpkin - instead of the lovely angel that she was. I rushed through the corridors of the hospital, praying with all my heart that she should be fine, and longing to hold her hands.

As I stepped into the ward, the first thing I saw was a magnificent flower bouquet that made my own look like a bunch of matchsticks. Then I saw Lucy, propped up on a dozen pillows, not looking quite as frazzled as I had feared, which of course was a tremendous relief. But what actually threw me was that there, in his ludicrous oversized suit and his best second-hand Gatsby shirt, was my friend Tim. He was sitting beside Lucy, both of them tenderly holding hands. The grin plastered across his ratty little face was wider than the Grand Canyon. Suddenly, without any warning at all, my throat began to itch, and I broke down in an uncontrollable fit of 'sneagles'.

An Unwholesome Trinity

James sighed and pushed the yellow folder to one side. His mind was abuzz with competing thoughts between his current work and the important decision he'd have to make later that night. A decision that could change the course of his life. At twenty past five, it was obviously too late to start working on a new case. But something kept him welded to his black leather-trimmed manager's chair. After all, he thought, apart from vegetating in front of the TV, there was nothing else to do at home that night - well, at least, not until 11 pm, when he'd be making that important phone call. So he opened the folder in front of him marked "PX11706 - Patrick Butcher".

It contained three sheets of paper. He pulled them out one by one and laid them side by side on his pristine blackwood desk, wondering which of the statements to read first. Fred's statement was slashed out in a hasty, spidery scrawl which, despite its apparent sloppiness, was still quite remarkably legible. Each letter leaned forward like a sprinter in a relay race. The spaces between the words were close together in some places and far apart in others, so that they appeared to be strung together like beads on a stretched elastic band.

The next report was written in handwriting that looked like commentary on an elaborate laboratory report, and the words had been imprinted with considerable pressure, so that James could feel the impression as he ran his fingers over the pages.

The last statement was the neatest of the three. His letters were well-formed, and his cursive script was upright, bold and confident - and no words were crossed out.

After a moment of deep contemplation, James picked up the first statement and began to read.

I came out through the prison security checks around 11 in the morning, looked around, and savoured the warmth of the bright sunlight and the smell of freshly mown grass, which I'd missed for more than six months. I was about to start off down the long footpath leading to Plumstead Station when I heard Alex calling out from the blue Ford Escort parked across the road. Bert was next to him, in the passenger seat, wearing a pair of snazzy earbuds, listening to music on his phone. As I climbed into the back seat, he merely grunted in disgruntled acknowledgement, his expression remaining sullen as ever. Alex was more welcoming; he smiled and shook hands with me. If we'd been standing, it would have been a buddy hug.

"Free at last, eh? Must be fantastic to be out of that hell hole. Once we get you home, and you freshened up, we'll hit the streets in celebration."

"Sure," I said, and he fired the Ford Escort through the gates of the prison grounds and out on to the main road into the heart of Woolwich.

I was dying for a cigarette, but I knew Alex wouldn't permit me to smoke in his car. I like Alex. He's a decent bloke and he always tries to do what is right, although sometimes he can be a bit of a holier-than-thou.

I tapped Bert on the shoulder. "Didn't you miss me, old boy?"

Albert was a nerdy old goat who had nothing going for him except his knack for invoking pity. Fun and excitement were absent from his dictionary. He turned round and glared at me over his thick black plastic-rimmed spectacles and then, taking a deep breath, turned back and continued listening to his music.

We got to the flat at around 12:30. We stayed in the flat all day. I remained in the lounge, watching TV - I don't remember what I was watching - I was just sitting there, wondering what to do next with my life.

I didn't leave the flat at any time. I didn't go

anywhere near Beth's apartment. I didn't tamper with her car brakes, or do any of those nasty things the police officer was accusing me of. I've only just got out of prison after six long months for an offence that I didn't commit. Do you think I'll be foolish enough to get myself straight back in there?

Well, I don't know, thought James as he put down Fred's statement. He sighed once again as he considered the situation. The case of wilful vandalism could have held if a fatal accident had not occurred as a result of the alleged brake tampering, but since the charge was murder it was a more complicated matter. The whole statement was contradicted by subsequent police checks insisting that there was no sighting of the blue Ford Escort and that a man matching Patrick Butcher's description had been seen around Woolwich train station just about the same time.

James' professional deliberations were interspersed with thoughts of his uncle's offer. His mind was in multitask mode, the rigorous process of "cost and benefit analysis" churning away in the background. He'd forgotten all about Uncle Francis' nightclub dreams until three days earlier, when he'd received a call from the old man right out of the blue.

"Hey, Buddy, how's it hanging?" his uncle's jovial gruffness thundered down the line. He was calling from Sydney.

"Uncle Francis. Quite an age!"

"'Yeah, it's been - like - seven years…?"

The last time James saw him, he was heading for Delaware on a charity exchange program from which he planned to go to India. James had waited to hear from him, but there was no word for weeks, stretching to months and years.

"What's this I hear about you becoming a bobby? I had you down for far greater things, boy."

James started telling his uncle about how he was doing remarkably well in his police career, but the old man didn't seem interested.

"Hey, Jambo, remember what we talked about so many years ago - the nightclub business in Aussie?"

Of course James remembered. The old man would never stop going on about it, although James had thought it was just a pipe dream. Uncle Francis' dream was to emigrate to Australia and open a nightclub. And when he did, his best nephew James would be his right-hand man.

"Yes, Uncle F, you haven't..."

"You bet I have! I'm right here in the land of Oz, celebrating the purchase of a high street nightclub called *Glitters*. This is it, boy. We're going to have a fabulous time running the place. What I need from you now, young man, is to tell me when you'll be coming over to help me run the show."

James was silent.

He was making considerable progress with his work. In the past seven years that he hadn't heard from Uncle Francis, he'd completed his psychology degree at the University of Nottingham and embarked upon a promising career with the Metropolitan Police. He was considered by his colleagues and, more importantly, by his superior officers, to be ambitious, reliable and guaranteed to go far very quickly.

At times, he was even disturbed by subversive thoughts that challenged his impressive career progress. Perhaps there was more to life than a safe express route to the secure and settled future which he seemed to be accelerating towards. He was only 27 and he already headed a new post-investigative department, and even people who were ten years older were calling him "boss".

"James, are you still there?" Uncle Frank asked.

"Yes, Uncle. I need some time to think about this."

"Hey look, Jambo, I know you're thinking about your police career, but trust me; this club will be the top club around here. You wait until you see my plans. You'll make more money in this business than anything the police has to offer. And it will be a lot more fun. Think of the partying, the booze, the girls, and all the sunshine. Not to mention that you'll be a partner and carry on the good work when I'm gone and long forgotten."

James sighed, "Uncle Frank, I really do need some time. Can I get back to you on this in about two weeks?"

"Come on, sonny. This thing is hot, man. There are papers to be signed and orders to be placed. We can't just put everything on hold while you take two weeks to make up your mind. I must tell you there are other candidates for this position. I'm only giving you the privilege of first offer because you're my favourite. You're the top guy with all the right skills. You're cut out for this, James."

When James didn't reply, Uncle Francis went on, "Well, I've said my bit. I can only wait for you till next Friday. 8 am on Friday, that's it."

And that was it. 8 in the morning in Sydney would be 11 pm in London. James had thought about it the whole week. He'd confirmed that Uncle Francis had indeed bought the nightclub and wasn't just having him on. It was a tough one, and he certainly had to give it a good thought. But, at the end of the day, it was up to him.

James dragged his mind back to the task at hand. He put Fred's statement aside and pulled Bert's in front of him.

Why that rascal Fred was let out of prison, I can't possibly imagine. He should have been left there to rot. If Alex hadn't dragged me along, I wouldn't have cared to see him at all.

I'll tell you how the moron lost us our chance of a lifetime and cost us a fortune. The good-for-nothing, marshmallow-brained imbecile.

I'd only gone and invented the space hook, that's what I'd done. Absolute genius of an idea it was, too. No wonder there, of course, nothing less can be expected from one who bagged his MSc from Princeton and PhD from Cambridge. My masterpiece was the ultimate antigravity automobile braking system, an absolute gem of an idea that could only have been thought up by a mind like mine. My invention was in spontaneous geomagnetics and deep-space geokinetics, involving the kind of maths that'd make Einstein quake in his grave.

Alex had just completed his MBA at the London School of Economics and suddenly saw the light. "What you're sitting on here is a gold mine," he'd declared, as if I didn't know that all along. He boasted that he had the means and connections to turn my invention into serious money.

Fred, of course, would be an indispensable member of the team because of his legendary charm and charisma. Those were Alex's words - "Legendary charm and charisma." As far as I'm concerned, Fred is just a smooth-talking bastard without two brain cells to rub together. But Alex thought the eel would be useful to have around for negotiations and marketing.

That's how we all got together and worked on my idea. I tweaked up the design and polished up the blueprint. Alex put it through the patent office and established some lines of contact, and Fred blagged his way into the boardrooms, and got us noticed among the top players in the automobile circles. It was all going jolly well. Before you could say Jack Robinson, we were talking big bucks with CEOs in New York and Tokyo. Yes. Every motor manufacturer on the planet wanted a piece of the action.

Finally, I was going to get some recognition for all my hard work, perhaps a Nobel Prize was in the frame. Fred was full of fancy dreams. He was going to buy himself a yacht and sail along the coasts of Morocco. Alex would go into politics and become powerful and influential. He'd make decisions that would affect the lives of millions, and leave a lasting legacy in his name.

But the whole thing began to go pear-shaped when Fred started going out with Beth, the high-class chick who worked for Realtex Conglomerates. We saw less and less of him after that. He'd leave the flat at eight in the morning and come back after midnight. When we discussed our plans for the next phase of the project, his eyes glazed over and he yawned. I tried to convince Alex that we ditch the moron, but Alex would not hear of it.

"Fred's our front man," he said. "We can't get anywhere without him."

Well, to cut the long, sorry story short, on the day he was supposed to be signing the final deal with Toyota in Japan, we were shocked to hear he'd been arrested on the M40, close to High Wycombe, for speeding in his wretched Ford Capri. He had no insurance and was in possession of illegal drugs.

It didn't take a genius to work out that Fred had given our blueprint to Beth, and she'd dutifully passed it on to Realtech. It's fallen into the hands of the unscrupulous hawks. They fixed him, had him put away, and left us high and dry.

It served him right, of course. Considering the way he'd lost us our big chance, I think six months was far less than he truly deserved.

Anyway, as we took him back to the flat after we'd picked him up from Belmarsh, he was full of regret for what he'd done to us, promising to make amends. But I don't see how his taking revenge on Beth could have put things right. He'd have to do more than that, wouldn't he?

James jotted down some comments. It didn't matter how many times he'd read criminal statements, it was still difficult to maintain that professional distance demanded by the BPS. You couldn't help feeling sorry for people as they vigorously defended their innocence even in the face of all overwhelming evidence to the contrary. You took sides - you even still rooted for the charismatic villain. And sometimes the intrigue of their dilemma continued to live with you for days to come. Somehow, you grew into their situation and came to anticipate the next saga as if their life was your own.

The running of a nightclub would present its own intriguing challenges. James imagined that it would be an immensely exciting job that suited a part of him right down to the ground: that part of him that craved fun and enjoyment. Yet there was another part of him that sought stability and security. Saying yes to Uncle Francis would be saying yes to a life of parties, girls, drinking and unlimited fun. However, with that, he foresaw a delay - or total absence - of the settled life that was almost certainly guaranteed by his current trajectory.

But returning to this case before him, James modified some remarks in his notes. Then he added some more comments after consulting volume 26 of the BPS reference, which he retrieved from his overcrowded bookshelf. After that, he put the statement away and picked up the final one - Alex's statement, the one with the neat handwriting.

I can tell you for sure that Fred didn't do it. That night, we were all in the flat. It was his first day out of prison, and all he wanted to do was to settle down and get his act together.

Fred and Bert had an argument in the car, almost coming to blows. I had to stop the car to get Bert to calm down. But after that there was no further incident.

There was a knock, and we were surprised when we opened the door, and it was the police. I assure you that, contrary to the officer's allegations, we cooperated fully, and came down to the police station without a fuss. Bert didn't spit at the officer, and he didn't try to hit the officer's female colleague. Fred certainly didn't go anywhere near the woman's house, and he didn't tamper with her brakes. He was in the flat all along.

It's true that Fred can sometimes be a sneaky and irresponsible goat who shouldn't always be taken seriously. He's forever chasing after women and getting himself into unnecessary trouble. But in his heart he's a lovely bloke all the same.

Bert can often be a bumbling, incompetent, antisocial idiot with a closed mind, but he is not a criminal, and he has a great deal of respect for the law. He's also a very loyal person, and would work hard for the things he believes in.

I take personal responsibility for the way that things have turned out among us. For a long time, I remained aloof, and allowed both rascals to run amok when I should have taken charge. Subsequently, right from secondary school to this moment, well over forty years, we've been cruising, at top speed, on the highway to nowhere. But I'm sure that everything will be fine from now on. As long as we don't keep being pestered by the police or other authorities, we will settle down and make something of our lives.

James put the last statement aside, shaking his head in disbelief. What astonished him most was that, despite the differences in handwritings, all three statements were written by a single person, a tramp named Patrick Butcher. He hadn't even completed his secondary education, and certainly never got within a sniff of Cambridge or Princeton. As for his invention, no such thing existed as far as anyone could tell. He was just an aberrant layabout, a mere tramp with a severe split personality disorder. He'd previously been imprisoned for being in possession of a large quantity of crack cocaine, and then on the day of his release he was accused of tampering with the brakes of a woman's car, leading to a fatal crash. The woman's son was sure that he'd seen Patrick come out from underneath the car with grease on his hands. However, Patrick was later cleared as it turned out that the intruder was a different person altogether.

Patrick's file had been passed on to James' department for post-release assessment and recommendations. James had personally interrogated the guy and, apart from the state of his clothes, he seemed quite normal. He didn't appear to have any mental disability, and his behaviour was impeccable throughout. The probation officer, who was a brash Jamaican man in his late 40s, couldn't control his bewilderment. "The man is mad," he declared in exasperation, "How can one person be three people at the same time?" shaking his head incredulously he continued, "This is the worst case of split personality disorder I've ever seen! In my opinion, he ought to be sectioned at once; or the next thing you know he's a full blown mental case and a danger to the public. You never know what he may get up to."

But James couldn't see why he should agree with the officer in recommending long-term mental custody. After all, everyone had their own coping mechanism for navigating the complexities and uncertainties of life. Moreover, we all possess the same traits of "Alfred", "Albert" and "Alex" in varying proportions.

It was close to nine, and darkness had long dominated the skies by the time James completed his recommendations. As he walked down Coleman Street, he felt a certain peace. Deep down, he knew he'd finally made up his mind about his uncle's offer.

Farewell, Cruel World

Death   was   the first of the guests to arrive at the Gravesend cabin lodge resort. Upon opening the door, Tom was startled to see him standing right in the middle of the central lounge. Tom stared into Death's deep eyes and instinctively accepted the clammy vice that was Death's hand of friendship. Death's smile sent a tremor down Tom's spine, but he quickly realized that it was well-meaning - a smile he'd find increasingly alluring as he continued to see it over the course of their short spell at the resort.

Death didn't have to introduce himself. He had a mysterious presence that could be neither faked nor mistaken. His wiry, middle-aged face was etched with the essence of time, and his lips were pressed together in a   formidable   expression of profound gravity, but he often permitted a glimmer of mischievous humour to flit randomly across his face, though it could be noticed only by the keen observer.

Tom nervously introduced himself as the "events manager" and assured Death that he would do his darned best to ensure that he and his chums had a fantastic time at the resort.

"I don't know exactly how many people are coming tonight," Tom said, cautiously fishing for information, "but I've been assured by top management that no expense has been spared towards making your stay an absolute success."

"I'm afraid," Death replied, "I don't know how many of us will be coming either. I was tipped off anonymously about this reunion. I decided to come only at the last minute."

As Tom began opening the front windows, Death offered to help with his chores, since Tom had let slip that he'd be the only member of staff on duty during their stay. Tom thanked Death, but hastened to assure him that he could handle everything on his own. At that time, at least, Tom was still quite wary of owing Death a favour.

Tom was already starting to relax in Death's cordial company when Fear arrived unexpectedly. Tom had his back turned at the time, so he was caught totally unawares when he heard a high-pitched voice like a frightened child's.

"Hi there!"

Fear was in a dark green silk crepeline top and a

pair of brown, baggy trousers. Her small crop of black hair was whipped up and knotted at the top, giving her pale, oblong face a strange look, and exaggerating the size of her brown glistening eyes that seemed to glower suspiciously at him. Then, just when he began to feel uncomfortable, her face relaxed into a tepid smile.

Tom was quick to regain his composure and promptly recited his previously rehearsed courtesies.

"Of course, I had no problem finding the place at all," she replied. "I've been here a couple of times."

Fear declined Tom's offer to help with her suitcase. "It's okay, dear. I can manage on my own," she said. However, she still sounded out of breath. She wheeled her luggage past Death without a glance. Death didn't acknowledge her either, but somehow Tom got the impression they knew each other well.

Wondering who had brought Fear, Tom glanced out of the window, but there was no sign of a vehicle anywhere in sight.

Next, Tom went to check that everything was in order in each of the rooms. It was just as the proprietor had told him on the phone. The rooms were sparsely furnished, and the beds had already been made. The smell of old wood hung in the air and it was clear that the rooms were rarely used. Tom had been given specific instructions, so although he'd never been to the place, he knew where everything was and exactly what to do. The only thing he didn't know was the identity of the guests and how many to expect. He'd been forewarned that they were a "rather eccentric bunch" and, whatever he did, he was to show no sign of surprise or bafflement at their appearance or behaviour. In any event, he'd been assured that, as long as he played his part, everything would be okay.

Right until the time he'd set out for the assignment, he was still pinching himself. He couldn't comprehend how lucky he'd been to have landed such a fabulous job. He'd practically lost all hope on almost everything. He'd been unemployed for more than two years and had even stopped applying for jobs. He'd begun to get used to the dole money, and resigned himself to living out the rest of his days at the ground floor council flat with his rapidly ageing and increasingly despondent mother. It was already looking as if, with his lack of skill, intelligence, experience and motivation, shame and failure had become his irrevocable portion in life.

So he couldn't have been more overjoyed when the letter arrived. It was an offer for a job that he hadn't even applied for. And, to top it all, the pay was more than agreeable - better than any of the jobs he'd actually sought.

He couldn't wait to tell Sally. But when he did, he was flabbergasted that she did not take it in the congratulatory spirit that he'd envisaged. Instead, she was full of scepticism about the whole thing.

He found her attitude depressing, because he'd hoped that the announcement would certainly cheer her up and get him into her good books. Unfortunately, they weren't exactly "an item". But she was the nearest thing to a girlfriend he'd probably ever have - or any other kind of friend, for that matter. He was painfully aware, of course, that his affection for her would never be returned. He'd never had any conversation with Sally during which she was not trying to get away. She was always on her way to something more important or urgent, and Tom was often under the impression that she was not eager for them to be seen together. But he'd genuinely thought that his impending change of fortune would get him a spot on her busy schedule and perhaps lead to the romance of his dreams.

"I'm not convinced about this fantastic new job of yours, Tom. Nobody hands out a responsible appointment like that to a jerk without any experience whatsoever. Besides, I've Googled the name of the company, and I can't find them anywhere on the internet."

Tom's heart sank at the ferocity of her scepticism; nevertheless, she carried on like a runaway train. "Have they asked for your bank details, to send your wages? You haven't even signed a contract with them yet, and you're starting tomorrow?"

All that, when she hadn't even asked to see the appointment letter. If she had, she would have wondered why it was handwritten, and the envelope not postmarked.

Even Tom's mum was full of doubt and misgivings. And she hadn't bothered to ask for the appointment letter either. A more caring mother would want to show it off to her friends and brag about her son's success. Tom was far from encouraged by the worried look she gave him and the edge in her voice.

"Be careful, Thomas, won't you? Don't go chasing after shadows. You'll only get yourself into trouble."

Back in the cabin lodge, Laziness, Incompetence and Sickness were the next to arrive. Although it looked as if they'd come in convoy, chatting excitedly among themselves as they entered, it soon became clear from their conversations that they'd arrived separately.

Laziness had on a pink T-shirt with the symbol of a clenched fist. He also wore a pair of black trousers that drooped around his hips, revealing the top of his boxer shorts. Clearly in his early twenties, he carried himself with a nonchalant aplomb that immediately put distance between himself and some of his older counterparts at the lodge.

Incompetence followed closely on Laziness's heels. Probably in his late forties, he had on a dark grey suit and a blue and white striped cotton shirt. When he spoke, it became instantly obvious that he was a politician.

Sickness was a plump, glum-faced woman, also in her late forties. She wore a frilly green dress and a brown silk scarf, and she had a whiny, sulky voice that made you cringe and lean away from her when she spoke. It transpired during one of the conversations that Sickness was always actively on the lookout for a long-term companion, and even though Laziness was much younger, she admitted openly that he was her latest crush.

Sickness allowed Tom to carry her luggage to her room, which was the farthest away from the other rooms in the lodge, and they both chatted as he led the way. Once in her room, Tom quickly left because he didn't want to be there when Sickness opened her suitcase.

After Tom had finished attending to Sickness, the next three guests arrived: Honesty, Kindness and Selfishness, again in a convoy. All three of them appeared to be in a jolly mood and in their mid to late fifties. Both Honesty and Kindness had the good-natured, friendly face of a benevolent Santa Claus. But Selfishness, despite her apparently pleasant mood at the time, had a countenance more suited to grumpiness. She was a tall, chubby woman who spoke in a gruff, gabbled accent that took much time and effort for Tom's brain to process.

At 5 pm all of the guests were sitting in the large common room. Some of the blokes were watching the Indian Grand Prix, and the others sat at the long table making small talk. Death was asking if anyone could help him decide which mobile phone to choose from between the iPhone 4 or the Samsung Galaxy S2. He liked the iPhone but thought it was far too common. He didn't want to be just another one in the crowd.

"I'll take the Samsung any day," hollered Laziness from the worn leather sofa where he remained perfectly comatose. "The camera on that thing is awesome".

"You can't beat the apps on the iPhone," Selfishness countered. "There are over a hundred thousand of them."

"I have no use for a hundred thousand apps," said Death. "I just want a smartphone with a decent contacts app and calendar, so I can keep all my appointments in order. I'm tired of lugging my appointment book around everywhere I go."

At that point, the front door opened, and three more guests arrived. The first to enter was dour-faced, slightly overweight and in her early forties. She wore her ash-blonde hair in a short, bouncy bob, firmly clipped in place with her ears. She was Misfortune.

The next was Guilt, a man in his late thirties. His dark grey shirt had large patches of sweat under the armpits. He looked around uncertainly and smiled shyly. He spoke in a slow and thoughtful manner, some-times leaving his sentences unfinished.

Integrity, who was the last, was more amicable than the other two. Although he was casually dressed in a white short-sleeved shirt and black cotton trousers, he looked a lot more graceful than Incompetence, who was more formally attired. He seemed quite friendly, but Tom still kept some distance, because he felt that to be in Integrity's excellent company he had to be on his best behaviour.

The three newcomers put away their luggage and quickly blended with the rest of the party. It was all going exceedingly well. Incompetence and Selfishness struck up an unlikely alliance with Integrity. They were both taking turns bragging about their charity work. It was obvious that they were trying to outdo each other in their desperate attempt to impress Integrity.

Sickness was sulking in the corner. She was annoyed because, despite her best efforts with her make-up and cologne, Laziness was not giving her any attention. Instead, he was flirting outrageously with Misfortune who, once she'd cheered up, seemed to possess a sort of charm.

Fear and Guilt had struck up an astounding chemistry, and they got on like a house on fire, chatting away like long-lost siblings.

Presently, Incompetence, in one final futile gesture to impress Integrity, offered to cook dinner for the entire crew. Tom showed him to the kitchen where everything was already in place. Incompetence stood uncertainly in the middle of the vast, cluttered kitchen for a while and then told Tom not to worry, and that he could manage on his own. Tom left the kitchen reluctantly, resolving to check up on Incompetence every so often.

When Tom returned to the lounge, Integrity pulled him aside and patted him on the shoulder. "You are doing a terrific job around here. Well done. Keep up the good work."

"Thanks, sir," Tom replied, feeling immensely pleased with himself for once.

Everything remained in order at the lodge until about 7:30 pm, when there was a loud noise outside. Fear's face turned white as a sheet and she shivered with fright.

Tom crossed the room and embraced her.

"Th-th-thanks…" she whimpered.

Everyone else rushed to the window only to find the wheelie bins on their sides and their contents scattered all over the cobbled driveway. Later, the culprit was seen walking towards the front door.

"Oh no!" Death groaned when he saw who had just arrived. It was Insanity, renowned for her disruptiveness and foul temper. She was a slim, middle-aged woman with the fierce countenance of a demon princess and a shrill, loud voice. She had on a purple blouse and a pair of black slacks. Her hair, dyed flaming red, spilled over her shoulders and flowed down her back like a river of blood. Her eyes flashed with mischief and evil intent as they peered from beneath her copious brows.

Death whispered to Tom, "Whatever you do, don't look into those crazy eyes of hers." But when Death chuckled and then winked at Tom, he immediately caught on that Death was only kidding, and it appeared that he didn't have any such awe or high esteem for Insanity after all.

As it turned out, Insanity had a few friends among the guests.

"Thought you wouldn't be able to make it," shouted Honesty from across the hall.

"Come on here, sweetie," Misfortune called, and embraced Insanity, making a loud "Mwah!" sound as Insanity got within her reach.

Integrity took one look at Insanity and turned away. It was the first time Tom had seen him show any sign of disgust towards anyone.

Fear and Guilt waved at Insanity, and she duly

waved back with the pretentious flourish of a Hollywood celebrity.

Meanwhile, Tom kept a safe distance and hoped he wouldn't fall under Insanity's intense search beam.

"Now, let's get this party on the road," Insanity declared. "Can we have some decent music around here?" Insanity was staring at Tom, who stammered, "I'm afraid, ma'am, all we have is the TV... If - if others don't mind, we - we can change to the music channel, if - if that is OK..."

But Insanity suddenly became distracted by something else, as her brows creased inquisitively and her nostrils quivered. "Hmm... What is that smell?" she asked.

It was only then that Tom remembered that Incompetence was still in the kitchen. Tom was halfway across the hall when the kitchen door burst open and Incompetence came running out, screaming as loudly as his choked lungs would allow. The tails of his jacket were on fire, and billowing smoke trailed his path from the kitchen door.

Instant pandemonium broke out among the guests. They ran helter-skelter and bumped into one another like billiard balls. Insanity worsened the situation by deliberately shoving her other colleagues about and making a hideous racket with her high-heeled shoes. While others appeared scared and confused, Insanity seemed to be getting the utmost mileage out of the crisis. The whole place was saturated with smoke and the noise of desperate feet, dragging furniture and smashing glasses.

It became impossible for Tom to reach the kitchen, not just because of the commotion, but also because it had become so hot in there that the heat was singeing his hair. It was clear that the flame that was already gutting the kitchen would soon engulf the lounge area.

"Come on everyone, follow me. This way, please!" shouted Tom.

Honesty was the first to leave the building. She flew past Tom at the entrance, still carrying her handbag. Laziness was next. Tom was surprised at his impressive agility, since he'd lain on his back for most of the time he'd been at the lodge. Others followed quickly, and even Insanity stopped fooling around once it was obvious that the entire building was going to be razed by the fire, which had now gathered considerable momentum.

Tom led the guests to the open field, away from the heat of the fire and the threat of flying debris. They remained there, huddled together for comfort.

Laziness tried to call 999 on his mobile, but he couldn't get any signal. The others had left their mobiles in the lodge, except Incompetence, who had his in his pocket. He'd forgotten to charge it that morning, though, so it was of no use.

"Where the hell is Death?" Misfortune asked with an edge in her voice.

There was a collective gasp as each one frantically looked around. Sickness began to whimper uncontrollably. Laziness held her hand to comfort her. Tom felt a dull pain in his throat. It was clear that they'd left Death behind. It must have been when they were all rushing around. Perhaps Death had fallen over, knocked his head and become unconscious. Tom was dismayed at the thought of Death lying there in the fire. Death was Tom's favourite among them all, and he'd become strangely drawn to Death since they first met. Tom sprang into action and leapt towards the burning lodge.

"No, Tom. Don't do it!" wailed Fear at the top of her voice.

But it was too late.

Tom was off like a truck out of control. He skipped over clumps of shrubs and fallen logs, and he bounded across the gullies on the footpath until he was right in front of the flames. Then, without a moment's hesitation, he leapt straight in.

Integrity heaved a mournful sigh. Fear shut her eyes tightly in horror. When she opened them, Tom was gone, and just at that moment there was a loud explosion as the flame flared wildly. He didn't stand a chance. What a horrible way to die.

"What?" asked Death, as he casually emerged from behind a nearby acacia tree, holding his black notebook in his left hand.

They all stared at him, aghast.

The poor lad had jumped into the burning building and lost his life all for nothing.

"The kid thought you were in the fire. He went in to rescue you!" Insanity shouted in a strained, tearful voice.

"No, it's not like that at all," said Death. "I assure you that I have never taken anyone before their time or against their will. You go round and ask, and you'll find that Tom already left a note for his Mum."

Death shrugged and then opened his notebook and crossed out his last appointment for that day.

About the Author

Olusola has worked as a part-time Math teacher in a secondary school, practised as a civil engineer in the Ministry of Housing and Transport, toiled as a warehouse worker in a parcel delivery company, mucked about as a kitchen porter in a fast-food restaurant, tinkered around as laboratory technician in a University, and hacked away as a computer programmer in various organizations. He has lived half his life in Nigeria and the other half in the UK. This is his debut book.

Made in the USA
Charleston, SC
27 February 2014